# The New Life of Hannah Brooks

## Acknowledgements

Grateful thanks to Louise Aldridge, Robert Attwood, Eleanor Leonne Bennett, Claire Bowles, Danielle Boyd, Chloë Brown, Trish Chapman, Sue Eckstein, Helen Matthews, Samantha Pearson, Dave White.

# The New Life of Hannah Brooks

Rodney Dale

Fern House

First Published in 2013 by
Fern House
19 High Street
Haddenham
Cambridgeshire
CB6 3XA

www.fernhouse.com

ISBN-13 978-1-902702-31-5

Layout: istudio21, Cambridge
Cover image: © Copyright Eleanor Leonne Bennett, 2013
Printed in England by QNS Ltd, Newcastle upon Tyne

**Our purpose:**

This book explains to the general reader that being an amputee isn't as easy as it might seem. There's a tendency to think that when someone loses a leg, they're given a prosthesis, and it's back to normal – just like that. Such a view is often compounded by the media making amputee life look so simple. Our purpose is to assist understanding of the amputee world by presenting something more like the truth.

**Our quest for authenticity:**

"You can see the hard work, research and dedication that have gone into this book and I'm honoured to have been asked for some input."

**Helen Matthews**, author of *The Amputee Blog*

**Or as amputee blogger Sue Eckstein puts it so eloquently (tongue in cheek):**

"If I could go back in time I'd very definitely opt for CGI [Computer-Generated Imagery] rather than surgery for my amputation. The outcome is far superior: no post-surgical swelling, messy wounds or irritating phantom limb sensation. With CGI you get beautifully toned, tanned, symmetrical stumps with no scarring, cellulite, weals or bits of sticking plaster residue on them. You don't have to endure months of tedious, painful, exercise and walking practise but instead get to stride out in public a mere two days after picking up your perfectly-fitting hi-tech legs."

http://sueeckstein.wordpress.com/

To Judith
Always my inspiration

# Contents

# 1

## Hannah Brooks

Hannah and Tom had booked the early diving session at the Golden Splash just after six in the morning, and were cycling along the Tamthorpe Road in single file. When they reached the Chequers roundabout, Tom dropped further behind and suddenly a huge articulated lorry appeared from nowhere, and something – Tom didn't see what – caught Hannah and knocked her off her bike and perilously close to the back wheels of the lorry. To Tom, it all seemed to take place in slow motion; he saw Hannah slowly flying up in the air, then returning to the surface of the road, her bicycle landing beside her, and something he didn't recognise landing in the road on the other side of her.

In a daze, Tom dropped his bike and got out his mobile to call for help, but found it was dead. Meanwhile, the lorry continued on its way, its driver oblivious of the accident he had just caused. Tom had the impression of a huge letter E and an enormous butterfly painted on the back of it.

'Stay there!' Tom shouted unnecessarily, as he rushed over to Hannah, seeing her twisted bicycle on one side of her and the something that turned out to be most of one of her legs on the other.

❧

After the initial impact, the ground seemed to rise up towards her, and when the lorry caught her leg, Hannah felt a massive bump and was astonished to find herself in a brightly lit golden fairy castle; she had no idea what had happened to her and marvelled at the fact that she felt no pain, only a sensation of floating as her nose bled profusely onto her long red hair.

Hardly knowing what he was doing, Tom knelt down beside her, squeezed her hand and kissed her on the forehead. A couple of cars stopped, and one of the drivers went over to see what had happened; seeing a red-haired girl lying in a pool of blood, he got out his mobile and managed to get through to the emergency services; he remembered a picnic rug in his boot and dashed back to fetch it to make the girl a bit more comfortable. The other driver registered what had happened, and swiftly left the scene.

Traffic built up; when a police car finally arrived, one officer sorted out the growing snarl-up, while the other went over to Hannah and Tom, just as the ambulance appeared. Two paramedics leapt out, assessed what had happened, and lost no time in treating Hannah with morphine to relieve her pain, and oxygen and a saline drip to stabilise her.

'Good to see you,' wavered Tom, suddenly realising: 'That looks like a leg there … it must be Hannah's … [he had some idea that separated body parts could be reattached] … please don't forget to pick it up. Is she going to be all right?'

'And who are you?'

'I'm Tom Curtis, Hannah's boyfriend. I saw it happen. Can I come to Jimmy's with her … with you? I assume that's where you'll be going …?'

⁂

The paramedics were working on Hannah's injuries, talking to her all the while to keep her awake, and PC Wareham was taking details of Hannah and noting Tom's account of what had happened, including the huge letter E and the enormous butterfly he thought were painted on the back of the lorry.

In her golden fairy castle, Hannah felt remarkably calm,

oblivious of what had happened to her. She kept repeating to herself: 'I love you, mum,' desperately wishing that her mum were with her, even though Tom was sitting beside her holding her hand.

PC Wareham had moved away and was phoning Hannah's mum, explaining in simple terms who he was and why he was calling, knowing that anyone hearing someone's name, followed by the words 'bicycle', and 'accident' would hardly absorb any more complicated information. He suggested that Jill should make her way to A&E at St James's Hospital to meet Hannah as she arrived. As he busied himself with his incident notes, two new police cars arrived bringing specialist Traffic Officers to take measurements and photographs of the scene, and to set about tracing the E-butterfly lorry that had been the cause of the whole thing.

In the ambulance, Tom was in a daze. The accident seemed to have happened in slow motion, but everything that had happened subsequently seemed to have passed by at lightning speed.

In no time at all, they reached Jimmy's A&E where an orthopaedic registrar was waiting to assess Hannah. It quickly became obvious that there was no question of repairing and reattaching her left leg, and that what remained of it needed serious attention. Within seconds, Hannah was on her way to Theatre.

༄

The phone rang: 'Jill Brooks,' said Jill.

'Mrs Brooks?' said a voice. 'This is PC Kevin Wareham of Frimley Constabulary. I'm afraid I've got some bad news for you, but try not to worry ...'

'Bad news? What's happened?' Jill quavered, fearing the worst.

'Your daughter, Hannah, has had a road accident. She's on her way to A&E at St James's Hospital.'

Jill went hot and cold: 'Is she badly hurt? This *is* our Hannah we're talking about? Hannah Brooks? You haven't made a mistake? And is Tom with her?'

'Yes he is,' said Kevin, 'and she's being attended to by the paramedics. Tom's in the ambulance with her. I couldn't say exactly what's happened. It'd be best if you went along to A&E at Jimmy's.'

'Yes, yes, thanks for ringing me,' said Jill, unable to focus her mind properly on what PC Wareham was telling her.

Frankie, Hannah's younger sister, appeared: 'What's going on, mum?'

'Umm … Hannah's had a road accident. That's all I know.'

'WHAT? What's that mean?'

'I don't know – she's on her way to Jimmy's A&E … in an ambulance … with Tom,' faltered Jill.

'Who rang?' asked Frankie.

'That was a policeman called … I can't remember exactly what he was called, but he said that Hannah'd had a road accident … that's all I know, which isn't much. That's why I'm off to Jimmy's to find out.'

'Oooh! Han! Can I come too?'

'Yes … please …'

Hastily securing the house, they jumped into the car and made their way to Jimmy's.

'Have you told dad?' asked Frankie.

'When would I have had time?' snorted her mother. 'Anyway, dad's incommunicado at the moment. Somewhere in Seattle I think – oh, I don't know what time it is there. And wouldn't it be better to find out what's happened to Hannah first?'

'Spose. What about Olivia?'

Olivia was the eldest of the three Brooks girls. 'She's still Wainwrighting in the Lakes,' said her mum. 'Let's not text her until we know what to say.'

'We need to know what's happened to Han first,' agreed Frankie.

When they arrived at A&E, they were whisked away to a relatives' room by Juliet, the Staff Nurse who was expecting them. They found Tom already sitting there dazedly. Juliet explained that Hannah had arrived at A&E and been taken more or less straight to Theatre, and that 'the consultant' would come to see them as soon as she had taken care of Hannah.

A nurse came in with a tray: 'Would you like a cup of tea, Mrs Brooks? Umm ...'

'This is my youngest daughter, Frances,' said Jill to both nurses, unsure of what she was being asked. 'And this is Hannah's boyfriend Tom whom you've already met. We're waiting for news of what's happened to my daughter Hannah.'

'Miss Pembrey the consultant will come and tell you about Hannah as soon she can,' said Juliet. 'Or send someone. Right now, she has to do what she can for your daughter. I know it's hard, waiting ...' She trailed off.

'Yes ... thanks ... Did you see Hannah when they brought her in?'

'Only in passing,' said Juliet diplomatically, 'I was engrossed in something else at the time. I know she went straight off to Theatre.' She paused: 'Would you mind if I leave you now? You can ask someone to find me if you need me.'

'No, fine,' said Jill, 'you must have plenty to do. Thanks for looking after us.'

Jill turned to Tom: 'So what do *you* know about Hannah's accident?' Tom looked distressed and told them about the E-butterfly lorry, and the unknown motorist who had called 999 and produced a blanket, and the arrival of the police and the ambulance. He didn't mention the detached leg.

Jill tried to imagine the scene; Frankie was disturbed and said something unhelpful to Tom, who broke down in tears: 'I'm sorry, I'm so sorry …'

After what seemed an age, a tall woman came into the room looking grave: 'Mrs Brooks? I'm Ruth Pembrey, orthopaedic consultant. I've been looking after your daughter.' Jill introduced herself, Frances and Tom yet again, delaying what she was certain must be bad news.

'Sorry to take so long coming to see you,' Miss Pembrey said, 'but you'll understand I need to find out exactly what's happened to a patient before I say anything to anyone. And I'm afraid that you must prepare yourselves for bad news. Now, as I'm sure you know, Hannah's had a bicycle accident, and the good news is that I'm sure she's going to be fine, but the bad news is that she's lost her left leg. It became detached in the accident and although the paramedics brought it along with them, there's no way we could have reattached it. It was badly crushed by the lorry that ran her over, but I can assure you that if we could have saved it, we would have done.'

'Ohmigod!' exploded Jill in tears.

Tom sat quietly, his head pounding with a jumble of thoughts: what would suddenly losing a leg mean to Hannah? What would it mean to *him*? And to Hannah's family? How could he have – or Hannah be – a one-legged girlfriend? How would she get about? How would the other guys react to her? Would she get a fake leg? What would that be like? What would she be able to do – and not do – with one leg missing?

Jill felt as though her head were gripped in a vice. Then she ventured: 'So … what exactly happened? Is she going to be all right? What have you done with Hannah's leg?'

Miss Pembrey paused: 'Well … it seems that when the lorry knocked Hannah down it also took her leg off – but it could have been a lot, lot worse.

'So Hannah *did* have her leg when she came in here?' ventured Frankie.

'Yes, but not attached to her. The paramedics brought it from the scene, of course, but time was of the essence. I must say that if there had been any remote possibility of reattaching it, we would have worked on it … but I can assure you that there was no hope at all.'

'And so what did you do with the useless bit of Hannah's leg?' asked Frankie.

'Frankie!' exclaimed her mum.

'Don't worry … people often ask that sort of question,' soothed Miss Pembrey, 'they naturally want to know …'

'Yes,' said Frankie, 'it is – it was – a part of Hannah. You can't throw part of her away just like that.'

'Well,' said Miss Pembrey, 'after we'd examined the leg and found that it was in too bad a state to be reattached, it would have been sent down to Pathology, to see if there were any lessons to be learned from it.' She hoped that no one would want to probe further, and continued: 'I know this is a huge shock; a huge thing to take in, but the simple reality is that Hannah's lost a leg, and we have to look *forward* and face things as they are, and deal with them, and not spend time mourning the past and speculating on all the ways things *might* have been.'

Frankie burst into tears as the reality sank in: 'So you say Hannah's only got one leg now. Surely you must have made a mistake? Things like that just don't happen …'

Her mum put her arms round Frankie to comfort her: 'There, there. That's what Miss Pembrey *is* saying, I'm afraid, and we've got to face it, and deal with it, and help Hannah to face it and deal with it too. No good for *her* if *we* can't handle it …'

''Spose not …'

'So what exactly *did* you do for Hannah?' If this consultant were going to be so matter-of-fact, they might as well find out everything they could.

'Well, we examined what remained of her leg very carefully, and made sure that all the remaining tissue was clean, and had a good blood supply. Then we tidied up the bone in the residual limb … made sure there were no splinters … and now I want to get Hannah up and about and home as soon as possible so that she can get on with her life again; most of all, I want to keep her *positive.*'

'What's a residual limb?' asked Frankie.

'Umm … that's the part of Hannah's left leg we *have* been able to save. Still part of her.'

Jill's heart gave a little jump: 'So how much of her left leg does she still have?' she asked.

'The upper part of her thigh,' said Miss Pembrey, 'about 20 centimetres from the hip – quite a respectable residual limb for her prosthesis when the time comes.'

The idea of Hannah having a 'residual limb' for a 'prosthesis' sounded so cold.

'What's a prosthesis?' asked Frankie.

'An artificial leg,' said Tom, eager to show that he knew. Then he sobbed as he was suddenly overwhelmed by what had happened to his longtime girlfriend, and realised that they would no longer be able to share all the activities they had enjoyed together since they had first sat next to each other at nursery school all those years ago. He felt as though a part of himself had died.

'No left foot, no left shin, no left knee, only half her left thigh …' Tom intoned.

'This may sound silly,' Frankie ventured to Miss Pembrey, 'but do you think you could cut off *my* left leg so that I can share what Hannah's going through?'

'Oh, Frankie!' Her mum was shocked. The conversation had turned somewhat gruesome ... almost unreal.

'It's OK,' soothed Miss Pembrey, 'it's natural to say things like that when someone close to you suffers trauma, but you can see it wouldn't really be helpful to anyone in the long run for me to amputate a perfectly sound leg – or ethical for that matter. I can assure you that there's no damage to Hannah's personal areas, and everything seems to be nice and clean and tidy now. ... [If I don't say it now, they'll only worry about it] ... We'll keep a careful eye on the wound because of the possibility of infection, but we've done all we can for the moment, and Hannah's a healthy girl, and as we don't expect any problems, she should be up and about in a day or two.'

'UP? Whooo ... that soon? ... so ... now what?'

'Well, at the moment Hannah's in Recovery, and then she'll be moved to a teenage orthopaedic ward – Hyacinth – later. As I say, she should be up and about in a very short time, all being well, and she could be home in a week or two ... [don't want to be too upbeat at this stage] ... depending on how she gets on. I'll ask someone to let you know as soon as she's been moved to the ward, and you can go and see her then – though it will take her some time to come round from the anaesthetic ... and a bit longer to be with it ... and then she should go from strength to strength.'

'You'll be able to make her a new leg?'

'Frances ... I can't promise anything and, in any case, I'm not a prosthetist – an artificial limb specialist. But I do know we've got some brilliant people in that department, and there are technical advances all the time. Now ... sorry Mrs Brooks, everyone, but I've got to go back to work. Feel free to give my secretary a ring if you think I can help.'

Jill stood: 'Thanks, Miss Pembrey ... Hannah's lost a leg ... that's going to ... take some getting used to. For her and for us. I really can't think straight at the moment. Well, see you later ... and thank you for all you've done.'

The irony of that sentiment struck her, even as she said it.

Tom was also in a daze … Hannah's left leg had gone; she'd never again be able to share with him all the things they'd enjoyed together in the past. They'd reached the unexpected and unthinkable end of their road. It was as if all that had bound them together so strongly had been crushed out of existence by an E-butterfly.

They waited in the relatives' room, looking idly at some tatty true-life magazines, flicking over the pages, unable to take anything in. Tom shut his eyes against the confusion of the day, and found that he could see nothing but some hazy sort of picture of Hannah missing a leg that filled his head completely.

He burst into tears; then, overcome by exhaustion, drifted off to sleep.

When Staff Nurse Sue came to take them to see Hannah, Tom grunted, pretending to be deeply asleep. There was no way that he could bring himself to go and see her with one leg.

'Let him be,' said Jill. 'He'll be dog tired, getting up at five o'clock this morning and going through what he's been through.'

Soon her mum and Frankie were looking down tearfully at Hannah almost lost in what seemed an enormous bed; she was fitted with an oxygen mask, a drip feeding into a cannula in the back of her hand, a catheter for draining her urine, and another drain-tube from the remains of her left leg. Wires connected her to bleeping monitoring equipment; she was unconscious and breathing lightly; a thin blanket covered her, and it was obvious that most of her left leg was missing, a fact that struck them both like an electric shock.

They sat one on each side of the bed, sobbing silently, stroking Hannah's red hair, whispering to her inert form how much they loved her, and that everything was going to be fine. Frankie so wished that she could creep into bed with her sister and hug and reassure her as Hannah had done so many times for her.

Frankie and her mum were worn out. Still conversing in whispers, Jill decided to stay at the hospital for the night, while Frankie and Tom would go home to try and get some rest.

Having called a cab, Frankie collected a somnolent Tom and they travelled home in silence. Tom hardly noticed when he was dropped off at his house. They hugged and kissed good-bye automatically, as Frankie made sure that Tom was safely indoors before she left him. She did not then realise that it would be some time before they saw him again.

# 2

## Jill Brooks

**J**ill spent an uncomfortable night in a surprisingly comfortable bed, drifting in and out of sleep and dreams, her head full of Hannah's accident and what effect it would have on everybody, how their lives would have to change. Suddenly, Hannah rose up with both her legs, explaining that it had all been a mirage, then appeared in a wheelchair with all her limbs missing, then Miss Pembrey was removing Frankie's leg so that she'd know what Hannah was going through; then it was Jill herself losing a leg, and finally there they all were in a row of beds wired up to bleeping equipment in a room full of strange people laughing and joking and taking no notice of them whatsoever. She was glad to wake up, until she remembered what was now reality.

She found Staff Nurse Betty, and learnt that Hannah had had a comfortable night but was still away with the fairies. Surely that was not approved hospital terminology? Going to see for herself, she found Hannah deeply asleep and breathing lightly, still connected to various pieces of mercifully quiet equipment that seemed to echo her dream, which she still found somewhat disturbing.

She leant over and kissed Hannah, and then came face to face with Miss Pembrey on her morning ward round, who told her that she'd be keeping a special eye on Hannah, and that the nursing staff would contact her if there were any change in Hannah's condition that she should know about. Jill tried to tell Miss Pembrey about her strange and troubled night, but Miss Pembrey was not into dreams, and somewhat curtly prescribed rest and recuperation at home.

At home Jill found Frankie watching a DVD about Beatrix Potter.

'Have you rung dad?' asked Frankie. 'You really ought to.'

Jill's husband Martin was away in Silicon Valley on business for an unspecified period. Their marriage had been under some strain for a while, and they had reached a stage when they were wondering what the future might hold for them; Martin had been away such a lot recently and they'd begun to feel they'd reached the end of their road. What was worse, they hardly minded; they'd every intention of remaining firm friends and carrying on with some loose arrangement. Jill wondered in what way Hannah's accident might change their family relationships.

'I suppose I ought to,' said Jill. 'What time is it in California?'

She Googled a time-map and, as far as she could think straight, Martin was probably still asleep in his small hours. She decided to ring him at her tea-time, but she wasn't sure what to say or how to say it. Then she remembered that Olivia would soon be arriving home from the Lakes, and of course she would have to know as well.

'I guess we should wait until Olly gets home before we say anything to her,' she said. 'Suppose you were returning home on a coach with all your friends, laughing and joking, perhaps singing, not a care in the world, and suddenly got a text message saying your sister had … been badly injured. It'd be kinder to wait … wouldn't it?'

Frankie woke her mother at four o'clock with a steaming mug of tea. Jill's mind was a complete blank. Suddenly, all the events of the previous day and the disturbed night crowded back into her mind, and she broke down in tears.

'It's … incomprehensible, isn't it?' said Frankie, giving her mum a cuddle and putting her phone on the table beside her. 'But you can't put it off any longer – it's time to ring dad.'

Jill picked up the phone. When she heard an alien ringing tone, she got cold feet and contemplated hanging up but then, to her surprise and trepidation, Martin answered: 'Jill?'

'Hello … Mart … that you?'

Martin looked at the screen of his phone: 'Yes … Jill … is everything OK?' Why was Jill ringing, he wondered? He sensed that something must be very wrong for her to call him.

'Marty … I take it you're not in a meeting …?'

At that moment, she heard the sound of a child crying in the background.

'Who's that?'

'Nothing. What's wrong? Why're you ringing? Is something …?'

'Marty … Hannah's … in Jimmy's.'

'Oh, Lordy … what's happened now …?'

'Oh, Marty …' Jill burst into tears.

Martin was stunned. What *could* possibly have happened? 'What's happened? What's happened to our Han? Tell me …'

'Oh Marty … she fell under a lorry. And they've had to … remove her leg.'

'WHAT???'

'Hannah's lost a leg … most of her left leg.'

'Oh! … So … is she going to be all right?'

'Yes, they've made her comfortable. At the moment, she's still sleeping off concussion and the anaesthetic. It's a total shock … and now you know before she does.'

'What's that?' Jill looked up to see Olivia who had suddenly appeared in the doorway: 'What on earth's happened?' she asked, sensing that something must be very wrong.

'I'm on the phone to your dad,' said Jill, flustered, 'telling him about Hannah's accident.'

'What accident?' asked Olivia. 'Tell me.'

'Hannah doesn't have a left leg any more,' put in Frankie.

'Oh, my God, what a homecoming,' Olivia gasped. She slumped down at the table: 'Did you have a good time in the Lakes?' she asked sarcastically. 'How can this about Hannah be true?'

'She was run over by a lorry,' said Frankie, 'on the way to the Splash yesterday.' She paused: 'I know, it takes some getting used to. We thought it was best to wait till you got home before we told you.'

Olivia snorted, and Frankie went over to give her a cuddle.

'When was this?' asked Martin of Jill on the phone. 'It's unbelievable. Poor you. Poor Hannah. Poor everybody. I suppose I ought to come home and see how she is.'

'Don't put yourself out, I don't think that'll help … I'm sure you've got a full programme, and it's better you get on with your business so you can support us in the manner … you'll be home soon anyway … won't you? … [To Jill, the background noise of the child crying at the other end of the phone seemed to be getting louder and louder as her head started to pound] … What's going on? Are you in the bosom of a second family, or something? Who's that?'

There was a long pause.

'How did you guess? said Martin, matter-of-factly. 'That's Grace, you'd love her, I guarantee.'

'Grace,' said Jill almost absent-mindedly. 'Send me a picture of her. If there's anything else you ought to know, I'll be in touch.'

'Yes … thanks … give my *very* best love to Han, and tell her I'm thinking of her … actually, I can't think of anything else now …'

'Yep … I'd better go now … Anything else?'

'I'm so stunned, I can't … we'll talk again later, when …'

'Yes. Bye for now …'

'Bye-ee.'

Jill hung up and thought of all the other things she might have said. But they didn't usually communicate by telephone when Martin was away ... especially abroad ... and apart from the fact that Hannah had lost a leg, there was nothing else she could think of, apart from Grace. What a time to learn of her existence. Typical Martin, she thought. And yet, there was nothing like Hannah's accident for keeping one's mind off everything else.

As for Martin, apart from the stunning news that his middle daughter had lost a leg, he couldn't help feeling that his plans to wind down his original family connections had been sent off the rails.

'I must go and see Han,' said Olivia.

'She's not with us yet,' said Jill. 'I should wait until to-morrow.'

⁓

Jill was woken by Frankie with a steaming mug of tea. Frankie comforted her and persuaded her into the kitchen where they ate mushroom omelettes with sweet potato chips.

When things were difficult, Frankie always found the best solution was to cook something.

Jill recounted an edited and completely incomprehensible version of her unsettled dreams, and a more coherent account of her telephone call to Martin – omitting the startling news of little Grace. They discussed who else they ought to tell about Hannah's accident, and how to phrase the news. They wondered why it seemed so difficult, and concluded that reporting that someone had lost a leg was not dissimilar from reporting that they had died – and you wouldn't want to impart such unexpected and disturbing information too suddenly or brutally.

'I'd like to speak to Granny, if you don't mind,' said Frankie. She had a 'close relationship' with Granny Brooks, who was aging fast.

'OK,' said Jill doubtfully, 'but don't forget to ask her if she'd like to speak to me.'

16

'Will do.' Frankie went and sat in a comfortable chair, putting off the moment. When nothing distracted her, she dialled the number. It was engaged. She thought a bit more about what she was going to say; then realised that she had little control over the direction in which Granny – or Gramps – might steer the conversation after her opening line. She waited. She dialled again; this time the phone rang and Granny answered.

'Hello – it's Frankie.'

'Frankie. I'm so glad you've rung. I've got you some of that special marmalade you like.'

'That's very kind of you. I'll look forward to that. Shall I come over?'

'Yes, but not today. We're off to the cinema shortly. Have you seen *Manta Ray Murder*?'

'No, but everyone's talking about it.' She drew in a breath: 'I'm afraid I've got some bad news for you and Gramps.'

'Bad news. Yes. Ted's left eye is very bad now – macular degeneration. Thank goodness his right eye's more or less OK so far. We hadn't really wanted to worry you.'

'I'm really sorry to hear about that … not good.' Frankie drew in another breath: 'Hannah's had an accident on her bicycle. She's in hospital.'

'Well, we have to expect these sorts of things when we get to our age. But, surely, Hannah's quite young. Is it bad? What's happened?'

'She had an accident. She's lost a leg. She's in hospital.'

'What? What happened to her?'

'Umm … she had a road accident. It was a lorry. It took off her left leg. She's in hospital.' I've just said that, thought Frankie, tears in her eyes. This isn't going at all how I thought it might …

'Can they put her leg back again? They do marvellous things these days. Should we go and see her?'

'Not yet, I don't think. Would you like to speak to mum?'

17

'Yes please.'

Frankie handed over the phone with some relief. Then she burst into tears as she realised how her granny was losing her grip.

§

Jill, Frankie and Olivia had a look in the hospital gift shop on their way to see Hannah. They chose a cuddly cat to keep her company, and made their way up to the ward.

Feeling a hand on her brow Hannah stirred; there were tubes and wires fastened to her body, and aches and pains all over her. She felt someone squeeze her hand, and tried to look around as far as she could without turning her head. Jill squeezed her hand again; stood up, bent over and kissed her: 'Hello, Han.'

'Mum …?!'

'Welcome back.'

'Where to? Where am I?'

'In hospital … Jimmy's.'

Hannah assimilated this. There was a long silence.

'Oh! … Wasn't I on my way to the Golden Splash? … Owww!'

'Darling … I'm afraid … afraid there was a lorry. It ran over your leg.'

'OUCH! So what happened then?'

'Well … I'm afraid the lorry …'

'Ran over my leg?'

'Yes …'

'But it'll get better?'

'I'm afraid not, darling. Your left leg's gone. But not all of it. You've got about half your thigh left which will be fine for fixing your new leg to, Miss Pembrey says, and then I'm sure you'll be as good as new. Everything else is OK … thank goodness.'

There was an all-consuming silence as Hannah closed her eyes amid her pain and slowly remembered who she was and where she was; she gave a little sob: 'Are you sure? Are you saying that … that I've lost a leg? It feels OK to me. Well … almost. It certainly aches and throbs. But I can feel it right enough.'

'Yes … darling … You can get pain relief by pressing this button here …'

Hannah took that in. 'Here? Is it possible to OD? Not that I want to, you understand.'

'Umm … I don't think so … They wouldn't …'

'But I neeed both legs … swimming … climbing up to the diving board … playing tennis … cycling … just living.'

Hannah flexed her muscles. Could her mum be joking? Surely she wouldn't …? Hannah concentrated hard on her arms, and bent her fingers. She flexed her thighs, calves, toes. Her right leg seemed OK, and she could hear her toes rustling the sheet. The left leg felt … different. And throbbing like hell. She pressed the button again in the hope of more relief. Very odd. And yet she could feel her toes, even though they seemed to be knotted up extremely tightly and immovably, and only her right foot made a sound against the sheet. She gingerly extended her left hand to explore her body, found that her left leg seemed to become a huge dressing part-way down her thigh, sank back into her pillows and burst into tears again. Jill waited, suppressing the urge to burst into tears herself; she told herself she had to be strong for Hannah.

Hannah tried to speak: 'So what *has* happened to my leg?'

'Well … you see … you were cycling along with Tom, and a lorry came a bit too close to you and knocked you off your bicycle … and they got you here to attend to you just as fast as they could.'

'Umm … so, that's why it seems to hurt so much. But what have they done to my leg?'

'Well … Miss Pembrey was able to save enough of your leg to make a … residual limb … for an artificial leg to fasten to, so you'll be … umm … as good as new.'

Even as she said it, Jill wondered if it was the right thing to say

– or, indeed, if it were true. Perhaps Hannah wasn't yet ready to think about such things.

Hannah let out a strangled cry.

'I know, Darling,' said her mum, 'but Miss Pembrey doesn't think there'll be any problem with the healing process. Then, when your ... umm ... residual limb's ready, it'll be a lot easier to fit you with a ... umm ... prosthesis. And there's no damage to your ... personal areas, so she says.'

Hannah let that sink in. At last she spoke: 'My *residual limb* ... and when ... how long ago did this happen?'

'Well ... today's Saturday. And it happened early yesterday morning. You were on your way to swim with Tom, as I understand it.'

'Where *is* Tom? Is he here?'

'I'm sorry. Er ... we haven't seen him since he came in here with you after the accident.'

'Oh. ... So ... Tom's gone. And so has one of my legs ... the left one ... are you sure? It feels OK to me ... except that my toes are ... all sort of compressed and twisted and muddled. And it's throbbing like hell. And my knee feels as if it's out of place. When can I get up ... have something to eat ... go home?'

'I don't know ... I'll go and find out.'

The tension had reached an unbearable level; Jill had to find an excuse for leaving the room.

Olivia and Frankie stood by the bed while Hannah explored her body: 'How were the lakes?' she asked Olivia.

'Wet,' she replied. 'And while I up was there, I had no idea what was going on down here,' she said. 'One can't go away for a moment ...'

Hannah wanted time to think ... to come to terms with what had happened ... her mum was telling her she'd lost most of her left leg ... which was odd, because she could *still* feel her curiously knotted toes. Although her left thigh did throb mightily, and there was that fat dressing ... and the leg felt ... sort of strange ... Could it be some sort of sick joke? If only she didn't feel so helpless.

She could hear her mum returning with someone for moral support: 'Hello, Hannah. I'm Sophie. Staff Nurse.'

'Don't I remember you from when my little sister Frankie was in here with a broken leg a couple of years ago?' enquired Hannah. 'Hello Sophie ...'

'Hello Hannah.' She sounded friendly and warm. 'Now ... [she became crisp and businesslike] ... I think your mum's told you we've had to amputate your leg ... [well, not me personally, you understand] ... and now you're awake, I'll see if Dr Callender's around and we'll ... take it from there.'

'The joke's gone far enough. I'm too tired for this sort of thing. Can't you just ... Hey!'

Sophie had gently turned back the thin blanket covering Hannah: 'I'm sorry, Hannah. It's true. You can see ... [Hannah pressed the button for more pain relief] ... Ah! I see you've found the PCA.'

Hannah looked down at the dressing – white bandages and padding secured with pink adhesive tape – and realised with a jolt that her left leg was now indeed just half a thigh. She let out another strangled cry, and burst into tears again.

'There, there ... Mrs Brooks?'

Her mum went to comfort Hannah, pulling the blanket back over her: 'It's all right, darling. I know it's a shock. But we've got to be positive ... [she turned to Sophie] ... What's PCA?'

Sophie became businesslike again: 'Patient Controlled Analgesia. I'll just go and let Dr Callender know you're with us again.'

'Dr Callender?'

'He's Miss Pembrey's orthopaedic registrar you come under.'

'Come under? Like a lorry?'

'Umm ...'

'Who's this Miss Pembrey you keep talking about?'

'The orthopaedic consultant who's been looking after you.'

'Do I need looking after? And can't I get up?'

'I should think so … as soon as you've seen the physio. That's Dolores Mayfield. She'll be on hand to help you get up and transfer from bed to chair and back and start you mobilising again.'

'Umm …'

'Yes. But just now we'll have to wait for Dr Callender. I'll page him and tell him you're awake, and he'll be round very soon. And I'll let Miss Pembrey know as well; she wanted to be kept informed of your progresss.'

'Right-oh. Thanks.'

Hannah lay in her bed feeling strange as she was now beginning to realise that she had a residual limb, and it was throbbing. She felt as though events were unfolding in some sort of parallel universe, or as though she were looking at what was happening through the wrong end of a telescope. She closed her eyes, her head seeming to be going round and round. Her mum sat quietly, waiting, thinking about what had been going on: 'Do you remember a policeman? Kevin Wareham?'

'Yes, yes. Was he the policeman who appeared beside me when I was lying in the road and Tom was there and we had a chat and I gave him your telephone number and then the ambulance came, and he said he was going to ring you and tell you what had happened. I didn't really have a clue what had happened. I hope he didn't scare you; freak you out.'

'No, he didn't say *exactly* what had happened – just that you'd had a road accident and were going off to A&E here, and he suggested that we came here to meet you. And of course when we got here, it wasn't until Miss Pembrey came to see us after … seeing to your leg, that we found out what had happened to you, and I must say it was a shock and a half. One minute your daughter's "had an accident", and the next you learn she's an amputee. No way you'd ever guess. The very last thing you expect. How does it feel … if that isn't a silly question?'

'Umm …'

Suddenly, a white-coated figure appeared, giving Hannah an excuse not to reply: 'Hello Hannah, Mrs Brooks. I'm Dr Callender.'

'Dr Callender. Very glad … to meet you. Hannah's wanting to be up and about.'

'That's very good to hear, but all in good time. We mustn't rush it. How're you feeling, Hannah?'

Hannah looked at him: 'How would *you* feel if you'd just woken up and found you were most of a leg short?'

'Umm … yes. It must be …'

'Yes it is. *And* I ache all over … [Hannah tried to smile to take the edge off her sharpness, though his manner did annoy her] … that road's really hard. Anyway, when do *you* think I can get up?'

'All in good time. The physio'll get you up soon and get you walking.'

'Hopping. *Thank you very much.* And when will the pain go away?'

Dr Callender avoided the question: 'When your residual limb's properly healed we'll fix you up with a new leg. Have you seen your stump yet?'

'My what?'

'Your residual limb. Sometimes it's called a stump. You need to get used to having a stump. Say "stump".'

'Stump. … I've only seen it like it is here, buried in dressings.'

'Right,' said Dr Callender, 'let's have a look.'

Jill wasn't sure she was ready for this: 'Would you like me to get you some sweets or something?' she asked Hannah as an excuse to leave the ward, and go and explore the Friends' Shop, taking Frankie and Olivia with her.

Dr Callender asked Sophie to remove the dressings so that Hannah could begin to become familiar with what her stump looked like. He suggested that she should massage it as firmly as she could; a little bit harder day by day: 'The more your brain comes to appreciate and accept how your body has changed shape, the fewer phantom feelings there should be,' he said. 'At least, that's the theory.'

'Phantom feelings?' queried Hannah.

'It's when you can feel a part of you that's not there any more as if it *was* still there,' said Dr Callender.

'Ah! I've had some of that,' said Hannah.

'Phantom feelings shouldn't be too much of a worry,' continued Dr Callender, 'phantom *pain* can be more … troublesome.' He seemed to choose his words carefully. 'Can you move your stump around without pain?'

Hannah tried moving her stump in various directions as she gently massaged it, until the pain got too overwhelming. Nevertheless the exercise made her feel better, as if she was actually doing something.

'That's really good,' said Dr Callender. 'You should try and do that two or three times every day.'

'That'll help to pass the time,' said Hannah wryly.

Dr Callender ignored her. 'Now,' he said, 'do you have any questions?' But at that moment, his bleep went off, giving her no chance to ask any; he continued: 'If so, perhaps you'd save them for to-morrow – I've got to go now. Sorry.' And he was gone.

Staff Nurse Sophie appeared with a small trolley and re-dressed Hannah's stump, before tidying the bedclothes and leaving.

Alone, Hannah was able to lie back and begin to absorb what had happened to her. Her left hand strayed down again to explore the dressing protecting the throbbing end of her shortened left leg. There was no doubt about it – her left leg had gone – she was an O-L-er – someone with One Leg.

Now she felt even more detached and unreal lying in this bed than she had when she was lying on the road, not to say stiffer and more bruised. She peeped under the bedclothes once again to confirm that her leg was missing, realising that the longer she lay still in bed, the more the phantom sensation enabled her to pretend she still had two legs.

She settled down for a good rest, to be interrupted by obs rounds, floods of pain, and the comings and goings of her mum returning with a bag of boiled sweets. Her sisters, who found they could get less and less sense out of Hannah, went back to Victoria House. As her mum sat by the bed holding her hand, Hannah suddenly reared up, vomited and sank back weeping. Jill rang the alarm; Staff Nurse Wendy arrived almost immediately, took in what had happened, and went to fetch an auxiliary with a cleaning-up trolley. Her mum stroked Hannah's brow: 'She's very hot,' she said. Staff Nurse Wendy agreed, noting Hannah's obs and reporting to Sister, who immediately arranged a blood test.

As soon as the results of the test indicated an infection, Miss Pembrey appeared and rang to see if there were a theatre free. In no time at all, porters Jack and Donnie came to wheel Hannah to theatre. Seeing Hannah go, her mum couldn't help feeling a pang of fear – what was going on?

'Miss Pembrey's examining Hannah's wound,' explained Sister. 'And she'll attend to any infection and take a swab so that we can identify what infection it is we have to treat.'

Stunned, Jill continued to sit by Hannah's now-empty bed space. A petite white-jacketed physio arrived with a wheelchair and a walking frame, only to find that her expected patient had flown. She introduced herself as Dolores Mayfield, who'd be looking after Hannah and getting her to start transferring from bed to chair and back as soon as she was able to do so.

'I don't know what clothes Hannah has here,' Dolores ventured, 'but it would be helpful if she has some underwear, and a couple of pairs of shorts, and a T-shirt or two ... and a comfortable, well-fitting shoe – perhaps a trainer. It all makes physio easier.'

'So how long will it be before Hannah's ... umm ... walking again?' asked Jill.

'Oh, she won't have a prosthesis for a month or two yet,' said Dolores.

'Well, she can come home on crutches, can't she?'

'We'll have to see how she gets along,' said Dolores cautiously. 'It may be better for her to use a wheelchair when she gets home.'

Jill suspected that life in a wheelchair wouldn't go down very well with Hannah, but she kept silent. They took leave of one another and Dolores left the mobility equipment in Hannah's corner and hurried off.

Jill had begun to see that getting Hannah up and walking was not going to be straightforward.

෨෨

At length, Miss Pembrey came in and sat down with Jill: 'Hannah's back in Recovery now,' she said, 'and she'll soon be back here. She's on antibiotics – and the pain relief of course, and I'll be keeping a close eye on her wound. Hope and pray. I think you should go home and get some rest. You can't do anything to help her at the moment.' They talked on for a little while before parting.

As she drove home, Jill mused on the way Hannah's accident had affected – and would affect – all their lives. She found Frankie sitting alone at the kitchen table skimming through a pile of newspapers and magazines.

'Hi, Frankie. Just got back from Jimmy's ... Hannah's doing fine, but Miss Pembrey's had to attend to her ... umm ... residual limb because of some infection.'

'Oh no! So ... what does that mean? What can we do to help?'

'Nothing, except be around for Han, when she needs us. Miss Pembrey was telling me how there's a danger that the hospital staff can get too familiar with their patients' problems – they've seen it all before – and they forget that patients' families are almost certain to find it something very new to contend with … something they've never come across before … in this case someone – Hannah – losing a leg. The staff may seem to act in a blasé way towards the patient, forgetting how new it all is to her and to her family.'

'Umm …'

'And of course it's difficult to …'

Frankie looked very upset and Jill wished that Olivia could be there too. She stretched her arms out to Frankie and embraced her with a sob: 'I keep having to remember that we must accept things as they *are*. Never mind the reasons – there aren't any. And never mind all the myriad of ways it *might* have been. It's like it is. Han's lost a leg, and she's not out of the woods yet, far from it. We've got to try and accept this and find ways of moving ahead, for Hannah. For all of us. Don't you see?'

Her mum released her embrace, and gave Frankie a couple of tissues to dab her eyes with as Olivia walked in: 'What's going on now? How's Han? I just can't get my head round what's happened to her.'

Jill explained, and then they all fell very quiet, thinking of Hannah and the infection and hoping that everything would soon be under control.

୨୦

When Jill next rang Hyacinth, the news was not good; she could visit if she wished, but it might be better to wait until the next day. They all had a good cry and a cup of tea.

Jill was trying to not to think about the implications of Hannah's recent operation until she knew more about it. She leafed through a women's magazine, wondering how the various models would fare if they were to lose a leg – or rather what sorts of clothes Hannah could wear when she got back to whatever version of normal was ahead of her.

Then she fell to wondering about models with one leg, and whether there were catwalk amputees, and what fashions there might be for Hannah in due time.

Frankie remembered that the crutches she had had when she broke her leg a couple of years before were still in the umbrella rack in the utility room. Thank heavens they'd not got round to returning them to Jimmy's – she could find out something of what Hannah might have to contend with. She went and fetched them and made her way to her bedroom, where she sat on her bed with her left leg bent under her. What would it be like having one leg? As it was, she could hardly recall what it felt like with one leg in a cast. She bent her left leg up as tightly as she could by sitting on it, and then carefully wound a long scarf round and round it and safety-pinned the end to keep it in position. Standing up was the first hurdle, which she overcame with some difficulty. But then she found she couldn't reach the crutches, and flopped back on to the bed. She rolled over to pick the crutches up; then rolled back and stood up again – a little easier this time. Now she positioned the crutches ready to walk. Putting her weight on them, she rather awkwardly hopped her right foot forward. After her weeks of broken leg experience, she was surprised that her attempt to walk with crutches was no longer as easy as she'd imagined it would be. She stepped the crutches forward, tripped, and fell over, banging her left knee quite painfully.

She lay rubbing her knee and appreciating some of the problems

Hannah might encounter – except that she wouldn't have a left knee to bang. Nor would she be able to unwind a scarf and revert to the two-legged state. Not quite knowing how she achieved it, Frankie managed to stand up again and take a few rather more satisfactory steps. She went out on to the landing, and practised some more. She understood a little more of what Hannah might be in for, but then realised what a long way she was from having one leg, unwound the scarf and put away the crutches.

℘

Frankie went and picked up her laptop to look for helpful tips for her imminent driving test; somehow this exploration turned to cars suitable for people who had lost a left leg – not too problematical, she found.

Then she had a look for fashion clothes suitable for amputees – again with a view to cheering up Hannah, but without much success. She found an amputee fashion parade but then moved on to artificial limbs for people who had lost a leg, refined her search to losing a lower limb above the knee, and soon found that she was entering a new world with its own technical vocabulary; she was dealing with a prosthesis for a transfemoral amputation or, more specifically in Hannah's case, an LAK amputee.

She thought that the least she could do was to try to be one jump ahead of everything Hannah would need to know about over the coming weeks.

℘

Frankie had just had her pre-test driving lesson, and was waiting in the test centre for her examiner to make an appearance. Sure enough, spot on 11.32am, the examiner appeared, a tall, lanky man of about fifty, with a balding head, wearing a brown V-neck jumper with brown tweed trousers, and carrying a clipboard with papers.

'Frances Brooks,' he called out, and they made their way to the car. On the way, Mr Langford asked Frankie if she could read a number plate on a distant vehicle – all that was technically necessary to make sure that her eyesight was OK for driving.

They got into the car; Frankie did the DSSSM check – Doors, Seat, Steering, Seatbelt, Mirrors. Mr Langford nodded, and signalled for Frankie to continue. Frankie checked that the gear was in neutral, and that the parking brake was on, before starting the engine. She then depressed the clutch, put the car into first gear, applied the gas, found the biting point of the clutch, checked the mirrors, released the parking brake, and the car started to move forward.

So began what seemed to be the longest forty minutes of Frankie's life so far. She reversed round a corner, avoided pedestrians who seemed intent on ignoring her presence, did an emergency stop, negotiated roundabouts and satisfactorily performed the manoeuvres of parallel parking and turning the car in the road, all the while keeping to the speed limit, glancing overtly in the mirrors, and keeping the correct line on the carriageway.

At last they arrived back at the test centre, and Mr Langford asked Frankie to reverse into a parking bay. With nerves of steel, she lined up the car and reversed into the bay. The moment of truth: Frankie took a deep breath as Mr Langford opened the car door and looked down to check that they were well placed within the road markings. The car was sitting correctly and perfectly within the lines. Frankie exhaled.

Mr Langford returned to his clipboard, nodding, humming and ahh-ing. Finally, he turned to Frankie, and put out his hand. Joyously thinking she was being congratulated on passing, Frankie shook his hand, but Mr Langford said crisply: 'May I have a look at your provisional licence please?'

Embarrassed by her mistake, Frankie handed her licence to Mr Langford, who nodded, hummed, and handed it back to her. He ticked a few more boxes on his sheet, and handed it over to Frankie: 'Congratulations Frances, I'm pleased to say you've passed.'

'Oh my! ... That's *awesome! Thank you*!'

'My pleasure. *You* were the one driving! Now, you'll need to send this off to the DVLA so that you can apply for your full licence.' Then he handed over the Driving Test Report, and asked her if she'd like him to go through it with her.

He read through the sections, showing Frankie her marks for each, ending: 'Well done, Frances.'

'Thank you. Umm ... might I ask you one thing?

'Go ahead.'

'My sister has passed her driving test, but she lost her left leg last week. Do you think she'll be able to drive again in due course?'

Mr Langford made a suitably sympathetic noise: 'She'll have to tell the DVLA what's happened to her. But with the right car, if she's as good as you, she should have no difficulty in driving again.'

⁊

Olivia and her mum were in Granny's Cupboard finishing their main courses when they heard a jovial 'Hello, hello, hello.'

It was Clare Perry, an old friend of Jill's, whom they hadn't seen for some time.

'May I sit here?' asked Clare, sitting at the table without waiting for a reply and looking round cheerfully: 'Lovely to see you all again. Perhaps I could shout you puds and coffee?'

A waitress had appeared, and Clare took charge, making sure

that everyone ordered there and then. She looked round the table: 'Hannah not here?' she boomed in her best PE-teacher voice. 'Nor Frankie?'

Right on cue, Frankie came dashing in waving a piece of paper, and spread the joyous news of her driving test pass, leaving Jill and Olivia experiencing a mixture of joy (for Frankie) and trepidation (for Hannah).

'So!' said Clare, 'What'll you have to celebrate?'

They sorted that out, and Clare realised that she still didn't know why Hannah was absent. She saw the looks exchanged, and softened: 'Something wrong ... with Hannah?'

'I'm afraid Hannah's in hospital,' said Jill. 'It's all been a bit much for the last few days. That's why we're here having lunch – to get away from it all and relax a bit,' she added.

'Nothing serious, I hope?' asked Clare.

'Depends what you mean by serious ... Hannah had a bad accident last Friday,' Jill replied as evenly as she could. 'She lost a leg. And because of some infection she's just had another operation on what was left of her leg, and we hope she's now on the mend. But you can imagine it's all been rather ... overwhelming. Hence our outing to-day.'

Clare sat open-mouthed: 'Hannah lost a leg?' she spluttered, 'Hannah? I can't believe it. Things like that don't ... How ...?'

Jill thought of all the replies she might offer to Clare's question. 'She was cycling to the swimming pool early last Friday morning, when she was run over by a lorry,' she said.

'Bloody hell, forgive my Norwegian,' said Clare. 'I ought to go and see her? Well, in a day or two perhaps?'

'I'm sure she'll welcome vizzies soon,' said Frankie. 'When she starts to get up and move about. Not too long now, I shouldn't think.'

'I might be able to help her,' said Clare, 'I had some experience of rehab ... when I was at college. I had a part-time job in a rehab department at Spelton; helped to pay the bills while I gained some experience.' She thought on: 'But of course I don't want to interfere … I'll stay very low profile and do nothing until …'

'I think that's very wise and helpful,' said Jill, with some relief; she could imagine Clare barging in and upsetting Hannah's physio and other members of staff.

'Which leg is it?' asked Clare.

'Her left,' said Jill, wondering why it mattered, 'A few inches down from her hip.'

'Don't worry,' said Clare, surprisingly. 'I've seen all this sort of thing before. These things heal amazingly quickly, and I can assure you that Hannah will be up and about before you can say Jack Knife. Once she gets a pair of crutches there'll be no holding her. Or she'll be all round the place in a wheelchair. I've seen it happen time after time. And I know artificial legs are amazingly good these days, and getting better and better all the time. Good to say, but sort of sad of course, that all these injured soldiers you get these days have put a real push behind artificial leg research, and the government is throwing money at the problem like water. They'll fit Hannah up with an artificial leg as soon as she's ready, and she'll be as good as new.'

Jill sat in silence. She had a feeling that Clare was talking nonsense, but couldn't be sure, and in any case Clare had come and plonked herself down at their table so it would be somewhat rude to argue with her.

They finished their puddings and had coffee, all somewhat quieter than usual.

※

After shopping, Frankie felt she needed to visit Hannah – if only to share her great news that she'd passed her driving test. She explained to Hannah how she'd have to notify the DVLA of her change in shape, and shared the reflected glory of Mr Langford's observation that Hannah should have no problem driving once more if she were as good as her sister.

'And I'll tell you something else,' said Frankie, after she had allowed that to sink in: 'While I was surfing I had a look for trendy clothing for people with one leg, and couldn't find anything.'

'Why would you expect to find anything?' asked Hannah. 'I've been thinking about clothes, and I can't see why I can't wear anything I want. I'm not a funny shape or anything like that. It's just that I'm now an O-L-er. What did you think you might find?'

Frankie thought deeply. 'I don't know. I had this idea that there ought to be something specially fashionable for you.' Should she ask 'what's an O-L-er?' she wondered

'But why, for heaven's sake? Surely you should try to look unobtrusive, not stand out by flaunting special "amputee" clothing – even if you could imagine what such clothes might be like.'

'I see what you mean,' said Frankie. 'I'll have another look at the web pages and see if that's what everyone thinks.' She realised without asking that an O-L-er must be a one-legger – just like Hannah to make up her own term.

Frankie decided not to say anything about Clare's revelations; for one thing, she thought it was a bit early to talk to Hannah about artificial legs, and for another, she wasn't sure that Clare had any idea what she was talking about.

# 3

## Dolores Mayfield

On Jill and Frankie's next visit, a petite woman in a short white jacket appeared: 'Hello, Hannah,' she said, 'I'm Dolores Mayfield, senior physio, and this is Patsy Hamblin, one of my assistants – fresh from a course. She looked at Jill: 'And you're Hannah's mum; we met before … ?'

'Indeed we did,' said Jill, 'and I've brought in Hannah's clothes, as you asked.'

'Glad to meet you,' said Dolores; she turned to Hannah: 'I'm here to get you on your feet again.'

'Foot,' said Hannah, 'unless of course you can persuade my leg to grow again.'

Dolores and Patsy laughed slightly uncertainly; Jill sighed with relief that they seemed to have a sense of humour.

'Now,' said Dolores, bringing out the equipment, 'this is a wheelchair – as I'm sure you know. But what people tend to forget is that a wheelchair can be just as good as a prosthetic leg for getting about – much of the time. And this is a walking frame, or walker, to get you started on your … foot, but before you begin to use it we'll have to make sure it's properly adjusted for your height.'

'Something missing,' Hannah laughed.

'What's that?' queried Dolores.

'A wooden crutch to fit under my arm, and a parrot,' ventured Hannah.

'Aarrr!' said Frankie.

'We don't do wooden crutches to fit under arms these days,' smiled Dolores, 'and parrots are a completely different department. At the moment, all I'm doing is introducing the equipment, so you can relax for another day. But make the most of it, because I'll be along tomorrow morning to get you started in earnest. OK?'

'That'll be good,' said Hannah. 'But what about a pair of ordinary crutches? How am I to get about?'

'Hold your horses,' said Dolores. 'You're not going to be back to normal just like that, and we've work to do before we let you loose on crutches – assuming that they're right for you anyway.'

'What?? D'you mean? … What?'

'You may be better off sticking to your wheelchair.'

'Hmm … I don't like the idea of that … kinda gluey.'

'We'll see… You've a lot of hard work ahead of you.'

'I can guess,' groaned Hannah.

'How long before Hannah gets out of here?' asked Frankie.

'I've only just come in,' wailed Hannah.

'I can't promise anything at this time,' said Dolores, 'we'll know in a day or two, when we've seen what she can do.' She turned to Hannah: 'Now, I'm just going to measure your residual limb for a shrinker.'

'What's that?'

'It's a sort of compression sock to keep fluids from gathering in your residual limb and causing it to swell.'

She looked at Jill: 'And thank you for bringing the outdoor clothes, but then I remembered that Hannah might want to wear her own jim-jams, so perhaps you could bring those in too.'

'Wonderful idea,' said Hannah. 'The ones with tigers.'

'I surely will,' said Jill. 'Tomorrow morning.'

'About ten o'clock,' said Dolores. 'I guess you can be a great help to Hannah's recovery one way or another.'

Stating the obvious, thought Jill, anticipating a list of errands whenever she encountered Dolores – anything for Hannah though.

The following day Jill was at the hospital just before ten. 'How's it going?' she asked Hannah.

'Throb, throb,' said Hannah. 'Phantom, phantom.'

Jill passed Hannah her tiger pyjamas, and received a special kiss for the decorative kilt pin she'd found for the left pyjama-trouser leg. She drew the curtains round Hannah's bed, while Hannah chose her clothes for the day and dressed somewhat laboriously.

Dolores arrived crisply on the scene: 'Right. I've brought you your shrinker – designed to keep your residual limb firm and to stop fluid collecting as your wound heals. That's why I measured you yesterday, you remember.' Dolores showed Hannah the shrinker, and how to put it on, and explained how she should look after it.

'Now try sitting in the wheelchair,' said Dolores, 'don't forget, it's your instant prosthesis.' She showed Hannah how to transfer from her bed to her wheelchair and back to bed, and then back to her wheelchair again. 'I'll tell the nurses to keep an eye on you now that you know how to do that,' said Dolores.

After resting for a minute or two, Hannah started to propel herself back and forth to get the feel of the chair: 'Reckon I might take up some wheelchair sport – such as basketball,' she mused.

※

'You've got *me* today,' said Patsy. 'Dolores is off on a conference. Today we shall try an assistive ambulatory device – that is to say, this walker.'

'Where do you get these ... umm ... specialist terms from?' queried Hannah.

Patsy appeared to ignore her. 'You should use caution when you use the stepping patterns I'm going to teach you,' she said, 'as you need adequate strength and balance. Now, your affected extremity is defined as non-weight-bearing.'

'Not surprising, as I don't have a left … umm … leg – sorry, affected extremity,' said Hannah.

'Exactly so,' said Patsy, entering into a long description of how Hannah should rise from a chair to stand at the walker, move forward, turn, and then reverse the process.

Then: 'Can you sit round please, Hannah?' Hannah had been lying on her bed recovering from the effort of dressing; now she sat round gingerly and stretched out her leg so that Patsy could snuggle the trainer on to her foot and fasten it securely. Patsy then placed the walking frame in front of her, and she slid forward off the edge of the bed and stood up, slightly shakily, and grasped it: 'Cor, feels really funny without the leg. My balance has changed head over heels like crazy – how much did my leg weigh … ish?'

'Around 10 kilograms . . . ish,' said Patsy swishing the curtains open, 'that's the same weight as three or four bricks.'

For the first time her shocked mum and Frankie saw Hannah standing on her solitary leg; what remained of the other was hidden in her ample floral shorts.

'Perfect height,' said Patsy. 'Now …'

Hannah stood ready for take off: 'Ouch – the phantom's at it again,' she winced.

'Hang in there; let me look at you,' said Patsy. 'Great posture. Your pelvis is well aligned – unusual in the circumstances, is that. The pelvis has a tendency to drop down on the non-weight-bearing side. And of course, it's pushed up by the intact extremity on the other side.'

'Off I go?' enquired Hannah. She thought about what she needed to do. Put her full weight on her leg so that she could move the frame; then transfer her weight to the frame and take a hop so that her leg could catch up with it. She was soon hopping rather ponderously around the room, supported by the frame, which made its own characteristic clicking and squeaking sound.

'It's a doddle,' she said, 'apart from my new centre of gravity.

What now?'

She moved over and sat in the wheelchair to rest; then she started scooting gently about.

§

The next day, Frankie found Hannah using the walker much more fluently. Gone were the laborious movements of the previous day; now Hannah was swinging along as if she'd been using the frame all her life.

'I did a bit of scooting in the wheelchair earlier,' said Hannah. 'But a wheelchair's not really for me ... something to do with being at sitting-down height, I think, even though Dolores said it's fine when you're talking to children, or to other people who are also sitting down. But I've always talked to children standing up – well, possibly stooping a bit ...'

'And now they'll be asking: "what happened to your leg?"' Frankie put on a high-pitched childish voice.

'Very funny ... Anyway, when I transferred to the chair I found that I was a lot more tired and weak than I'd thought I was when I was lying in bed, with the phantom sensations playing around me. Not surprising, perhaps. And I haven't been allowed anywhere near crutches yet. Dolores says they're not as easy as you might think. I don't know what you'd do if you needed them and you were all alone.'

§

'Right then Hannah ...' Hannah opened her eyes and there was Patsy standing beside her bed holding a pair of shiny new forearm crutches: 'I think you've had a long enough lie-in today ... time for you to wake up, and get up and about ... don't want that remaining leg seizing up now, do we?'

'I'm awake, I'm awake!'

'Yes, yes, that's what they all say. I saw you snoozing!'

'OK, *OK*. I'm ready … I've already given what you call my stump a good massage, and my dressing's been changed.'

'That's right – remember – you've got to learn to love that stump. It's an important part of you now. Anyway, we're going to try you ambulating on these assistive devices today – crutches … [Hooray!!!] … much easier than the walker … lighter; less effort; should be easier for you to move around. But easier to fall, of course.'

'Awesome. Let's get going then.'

'Let me put this gait belt on you so that I can give you some support if necessary …'

Hannah had already put on her shorts and top for the day; she swung her leg round, felt her toes into her trainer, and stood up supported by the walking frame, continuing to get used to the lopsided feeling of having only one leg to stand on.

Patsy checked the height adjustment of the crutches and handed them to Hannah, who took hold of them firmly, pushed the frame out of the way towards Patsy: 'These crutches feel much easier than that frame,' she said, 'but I'm still trying to get used to this whole lopsided feeling. Not half strange.'

'Yes. But just let me adjust the cuffs now. These go right round your forearms so that the assistive devices stay in position until you slip out of them, see? Makes shaking hands easier, for instance.'

'Would that be classed as a manual greeting procedure?' asked Hannah naughtily.

'Yes,' said Patsy. Hannah couldn't tell whether or not Patsy was taking her seriously. Patsy continued: 'The cuffs also facilitate opening doors and hugging people without the crutches escaping your control. But it can be more difficult to get fat sleeves comfortably into that sort of crutch – when you're in winter clothing, for instance. Crutches with just half-round cuffs make fat sleeves easier, and it's easier to throw that sort of crutch away if you're going to fall … but at the same time you have much less control over that sort of crutch. But … once you get used to them, it should all come naturally. You'll be fine, I promise you. How do they feel?'

'Better and better as I stand here.'

'Right. Now take the whole of your weight on your sound extremity, and lift the crutches, and move them forward together eighteen inches or so – forty-five centimetres-ish. Keep them the same distance apart … I'm holding you … that's right …'

'Umm …'

'Now move your weight forward on to the crutches so that your sound extremity's free to move forward between them … then transfer your weight to your sound extremity and move the crutches forward again … see?'

'Yes. I think I see how to do it now.'

'And that's just the beginning. You'll have to work out how to handle the crutches when you sit and stand and where to put them when you rest them and all that.'

'I must confess I hadn't realised how much there is to crutch management.'

Hannah could only manage a couple of circuits of the room on her crutches before she started to wobble. Her arms were not yet as strong as they needed to be and, seeing this, Patsy sat her back in the wheelchair to rest.

'I *do* know how tiring it can all be,' said Patsy. 'Even for people who are already used to crutches … after the amp it's almost like starting afresh, because you have a brand new body shape and weight distribution to deal with – as you've found. Makes a big difference.'

'Yes, I suppose it does.'

The next day, Hannah set off for the gym on her crutches. She was pleased to see that Dolores was back.

'Have you had a good break?' she asked cheekily. 'I've been learning to use these ambulatory assistive devices while you've been away.'

'That must have been … stimulating,' said Dolores. 'You seem to be getting on very well. But today, we'll be using some of the apparatus in the gym here.'

'Hooo! What'll we be doing, then?'

'Balancing on a wobble cushion, falling over, getting up, strengthening exercises …'

'OK, OK … I get the picture. Now … am I going to be using all these things?'

'Quite a lot of them, but not all the time of course. You'll be spending time with the parallel bars as you begin to walk. And the large balls here are for balancing on, and the small ones for throwing and catching. Those exercise machines are for strengthening arms and legs according to the needs of patients …'

'Right. So what are we doing today?' Hannah sat on a wobble cushion, catching and throwing small balls until she became a little too confident and fell off in fits of laughter. Dolores helped her back on to the wobble cushion, all the while explaining the importance of strengthening core muscles, and making sure that Hannah was familiar with techniques that she must practise and develop: '… but that's enough for your first session. Go back to the ward now, and I'll come and fetch you again the day after tomorrow. Meanwhile, if you practise scooting around in your chair, it'll be good for your arms, and help you to learn fine control. And of course using your crutches will certainly help you strengthen your muscles. But be very careful and don't overdo it.'

Hannah dozed in her wheelchair. The refreshment trolley clanked its arrival and she awoke to find that Frankie was just coming in: 'Oohh! You're up,' she said.

'Yes, and getting better on the crutches,' said her sister, 'and been to the gym and all. Exciting.'

'So you'll be coming home soon?' queried Frankie.

'Haven't had a hint of a date yet,' said Hannah.

'One thing I wanted to ask ...'

'Yes?'

'Did you find out what they did with the bit of your leg they couldn't use?'

'It was more than a bit,' said the literal Hannah. 'It was most of it. But I'd forgotten all about that. Well, I don't need to remember. I suppose they threw it away, or made it into glue, or something. But Miss Pembrey says I've got a decent stump to fasten a fake leg to ... though she didn't ask me if that's what I wanted.'

'Don't you?' asked Frankie, surprised.

Hannah laughed: 'At the moment, I don't think I do. For a start, my leg feels as if it's still there anyway – the phantom sensation. And it's throbbing like mad. On and on and on. And what's the point of going through all this wheelchair and crutch stuff if I'm going to get a fake leg? I feel as if I've changed. So why do they want to make me look like I did before the accident? Let's wait and see what happens.'

～

Dolores was at Hannah's bedside again, ready to get her up: 'Good morning Missy, you've got me for another busy day today.'

'Good morning, Dolores.'

'We're off to the gym again ... gonna give you a proper good work-out. Get you working all the right muscles.'

'Sounds ... good.'

'You'll probably ache afterwards … but then it shows it's working.'

'I've no doubt of that! Sounds like a physio talking.'

'Hey Missy … cheeky little Madam. We *are* feeling chirpy today aren't we?'

'Yes … not bad really. Had a good long think to myself – life's not so bad after all.'

'Yes … fair enough. Come on then … let's get you sorted and off to the gym.'

Once there, Dolores directed Hannah to a wobble cushion again, and they spent some time throwing and catching balls, giving Hannah's muscles a good work-out: 'You need to learn these exercises to keep yourself in trim, and you should work through them every day when you get home,' said Dolores, 'and here's a list of the exercises with pictures to remind you.'

Hannah dropped the exercise sheets into her pouch.

As they rested, Dolores produced another piece of paper: 'I've also brought you this list of points to remember. I'm sure you'll take them on board – a lot of it's obvious, but I always think it's a good thing to have them written down.'

Hannah took the paper, read and commented: '*Take care on slippery surfaces.* Well, I know all about that; take care or you may get … or perhaps *lose* … more than you bargain for. *Make sure that there are no slippery or dangerous rugs or carpets.* That's OK … but we'll have to take up our tiger rug – I've always been afraid that it'll bite me anyway. *Never hop about hanging on to pieces of furniture.* I presume they don't mean that you hang on to a bit of furniture and then hop about with it – that could be some feat … *Always keep your crutches to hand.* Well, obviously they'll be where you left them … *Wear low-heeled shoes that will not slip off.* Or maybe just one shoe, if you only have one leg … yes. *If falling, throw the crutches out to the side and use your arms to break your fall.* All right as long as you don't break your arms. Or throw the crutches through a passing window. Then you'd be in the soup. Thanks, Dolores.'

Hannah dropped the paper into her pouch with the exercise sheets.

'Right; off you go,' said Dolores.

'Thanks, Dolores,' said Hannah again. 'Give my bests to Patsy.'

On her ward round Miss Pembrey, accompanied by Dr Callender and Staff Nurse Mandy, came to Hannah's bed: 'Good morning, Hannah, and how are you today?'

Putting down her book, Hannah grinned broadly: 'OutSTANDING!'

'Wow! Upbeat, eh? We'd like to have a look at your stump, if you don't mind.'

As Mandy turned back the blanket, Dr Callender's bleep went off and he disappeared. Mandy gently removed Hannah's dressing to reveal the stump of Hannah's left leg, still bruised and swollen, and somewhat uneven; Hannah felt the throbbing, winced, and found herself in tears. She lay there, feeling as though her throbbing leg were being squeezed in a vice, and not knowing what to think.

But then, she contemplated the permanence of her new shape, and she lay back on her pillows and looked at the stump with some interest.

Dr Callender returned in jovial mood, glanced at Hannah's wound and said to Miss Pembrey: 'Yes … it's an interesting stump, isn't it? Healing nicely.'

To Hannah he said: 'We'll soon fit you up with a prosthesis, and then you'll be as good as new.' His bleep went off again, and once more he was gone.

'Can we leave the dressing off for a bit?' asked Hannah. 'Help me to get used to my ... new shape. Why did Dr Callender say it's "interesting"?'

Miss Pembrey smiled at her: 'Well, it's not entirely smooth, is it? But it'll settle down I'm sure; you're doing really well. Now, have you any questions?'

'Well ... it's not hurting at the moment ... just that strange phantom sensation ... is it going to be sore ... painful?'

'At the moment, you're still on pain relief, but we'll be tailing that off ... You'll be surprised how quickly the wound heals. As far as I can see, it shouldn't give you any problems now.'

'But it is a problem,' said Hannah. 'When people say that I'll "be as good as new" is this really true?'

'Short answer: "No", but prosthetics are advancing by leaps and bounds – sorry. You'll be able to talk to our prosthetics people soon – when your stump's settled down a bit more. You've got your shrinker to keep the wound compressed and stop fluid from gathering there. Anything else?'

'Yes ... how many stitches have I got?'

'Forty-nine. They'll come out in about a week.'

'Umm ...'

'Have you tried walking on it yet?' asked Miss Pembrey.

'No ... is that possible? How ...?'

'I'll have a word with Dolores,' said Miss Pembrey.

⁂

Dolores appeared, carrying what looked like a metal frame, 'Right,' she said, 'Miss Pembrey suggested I tried you with the PAMAid – that's the Pneumatic Amputee Mobility Aid.'

Hannah looked curiously at this new contraption: a metal frame to fit over a patient's stump, and an inflatable cuff to maintain it in position. They moved over to the end of the parallel bars, and with Hannah sitting on a chair, Dolores worked the frame on to Hannah's stump and inflated the cuff to half pressure to allow Hannah to get the feel of it; then she released the pressure for a few minutes before asking Hannah to stand so that she could adjust the length of the contraption to the ground. Then she pumped the PAMAid up to full pressure and there was Hannah with the equivalent of two legs again, ready to walk.

At first, Hannah found she could not get her right leg to move as she wanted – let alone the left leg. She had to concentrate long and hard on getting her muscles to respond as she wished. Mentally exhausted, she managed to walk from one end of the bars to the other once, and then back again, and the triumph of her success buoyed her spirits.

As Dolores deflated and removed the PAMAid, Hannah said enthusiastically: 'I'd like to try that again,'

'So you shall – all in good time,' promised Dolores.

෨

Hannah was lying on her bed, airing her stump and wondering what to wear for her forthcoming outing, when Frankie came in: 'Hey, Han, I've brought you your medium-length green skirt and the short blue denim skirt, and another pair of floral shorts and a pair of green linen trousers, and a couple of tops, and some undies. Oh … and some … er … right shoes. You'll be able to get dressed … umm … normally.'

Taken by surprise, Hannah whisked a blanket over to hide her stump, but it slid to the ground, leaving her exposed. Frankie stared at her sister's new shape. 'Wow! Is that what it's like? Quite a … shock.'

'I guess it is the first time you see it,' said Hannah, 'and it takes a bit of getting used to. It's really quite … dramatic, isn't it? But you must have a good look, it'll help us feel more normal when we're together if you're familiar with it. And that goes for everyone else. I don't mind.'

Frankie nodded and looked carefully at Hannah's stump with a mixture of curiosity and sadness: 'It's a bit ... crinkly,' she said.

'I expect it'll change shape and settle down as time goes by,' said Hannah, trying to be cool. 'Anyway, let's have a look at what you've brought me ... Thanks, Hun ... that's awesome. It'll be nice to wear some zanzan clothes again. Must try some on soonest and see how they work.'

Staff Nurse Mandy came in with her dressing tray: 'Would you like to wait outside?' she asked Frankie. 'This shouldn't take very long.'

Mandy redressed Hannah's stump, and when Frankie returned. Hannah sat on the bed and carefully pulled on the pair of green trousers.

'What shall we do with the empty leg?' she asked Frankie.

'Let me ...' said Frankie, reaching for Hannah's left trouser-leg, pulling it up behind her, and tucking it securely into the waistband. Then she detached the trouser-leg again, smoothed its creases and pulled it up at the side: 'You could do all sorts of things with this ...'

'I reckon if you wanted to cut a bit off the leg to make it easier to deal with, that'd be OK,' said Hannah. 'But just with this pair of trousers for a start. Apart from that, I reckon we should wait until I'm a bit more ... settled, and then see how best to ... I dunno ... maybe try some longer tops to come down to about mid-thigh, and then trousers should be *problemy niet* ...'

'Yeah. Sure we can dream something up. Shall I fix this pair, then?'

Hannah nodded. Then, as Frankie got out her pair of scissors, Hannah suddenly shouted: 'NO! Let's just leave it dangling and see how it looks like that.'

Hannah pulled on the green top that came to mid-thigh, and

Frankie burst into applause. Hannah hopped over to grasp her crutches and take a turn round the room, just as her mum came in: 'Han, you look great!'

'I'd been wondering about having a loose trouser leg, and it seems to work,' said Hannah.

'What about pulling it up inside itself to make a sort of pocket for your ... leglet?' asked her mum.

'Great,' said Hannah. She sat on the bed to try the pocket idea.

'Reckon that's got my seal of approval,' she said, 'but I do rather like the ... shape of the pulled-up leg.'

As Frankie watched, she was recalling Hannah playing tennis, climbing trees, turning cartwheels on the lawn, cycling into Frimley, running upstairs, swimming, diving ... the active Hannah that was no more. She wept inside, and noticed that their mum looked as if she was doing the same. But through both their heads ran the thought that they had to be strong for Hannah; *she* was the one who was having to experience all the new things and do all the hard work while they – and everyone else – could only look on supportively.

Hannah's mum appreciated that Hannah's single leg must *not* become the most important thing about her; the most important family topic. It must not overshadow everything else; everyday life must pick up and continue as normally as possible.

As Hannah tried on another outfit, Frankie forced herself out of her silence: 'Have you had any thoughts about other clothes you'd like me to find for you ...?'

'I'll be able to think better when I've got more used to ... all this, and when I'm home with my wardrobe,' said Hannah. 'But ... how about my white shirt and green tie to go with that green skirt ... and some green and white stripy socks ... er ... sock? What do you reckon?'

Frankie closed her eyes and visualised: 'That sounds ... neat,' she said cautiously.

'Well … my top and tie are in me chester in me bedroom … and I remember seeing the sock … the socks … in Maple's window, I think it was. Could you get me a pair … if you don't mind …'

The three of them continued to chat about Hannah outfits, until Hannah broached the subject of her stump: '… I could see it was a bit of a shock for you to see it without the dressing, but I hope you're OK with it now … there're forty-nine stitches to hold the edges of the wound together, and they'll come out in a few days. Anyway, I hope *you're* over it now, because there's no way we can move into the real world if you're going to have hang-ups … That's how I am. We have to live with it.'

And Hannah burst into tears; a cue for Jill and Frankie to do likewise.

&

The following day, Frankie found Hannah sitting in her bedside chair wearing her frilly blue denim skirt. She looked at her carefully and then applauded: 'Great to see that you're not connected to anything now,' she said. 'Have they done away with all the wires and tubes?'

'They surely have,' said Hannah, 'and that means I can go to the loo like a normal … ish person, with one leg – like I want to now,' she added.

'Let me give you a hand,' said Frankie.

'How about a foot?' asked Hannah, abrasive as ever. She was soon standing supported by her crutches, but her new balance was hindered by the strange feelings she had in the rearranged part of her left leg, as well as the phantom sensations, which kept taking her by surprise.

She explained all this to Frankie, who tried to grasp what she meant without much idea of the feelings she was trying to describe.

'Anyway, how does this skirt look?' asked Hannah, 'too short?'

'No, I don't think so,' said Frankie. 'It looks longer than it did when you had two legs.'

'Grow, Baby, Grow,' sang Hannah as she stepped off to find a loo.

Accompanying Hannah down the corridor, Frankie tentatively pushed open a door marked **Patients' Facilities** to find a rather dimly-lit lobby surrounded by more doors giving on to showers, baths and loo cubicles. In went Hannah, only to be brought up short by the sight of a one-legged girl on crutches coming out of the gloom towards her. She was amazed to see that the girl was wearing a frilly blue denim skirt just like hers. She stopped and stared; it took her a little time to realise that she was actually looking at her own reflection in a wall mirror – the girl was *her*! So *that* was what she now looked like to other people. For the first time, she realised what 'being disabled' meant. Previously, it had been something vague that applied only to other people. Now it was an adjective that applied to her. Her stump was throbbing, her arms were tired, her wrists ached, her palms were sore. Her head started to swim; suddenly she felt like a dishcloth; she managed to slip out of her crutches and discard them safely as she crumpled into a wet patch on the floor, managing to keep her throbbing stump away from the impact.

'Han!! Are you OK?' choked a surprised and worried Frankie. 'Hang on, I'll get help.'

She rushed out to fetch a wheelchair for Hannah and grab a passing nurse: 'Help! It's Hannah … she's collapsed in the Patients' Facilities …'

Hannah was hoisted brusquely into the wheelchair, made comfortable, and then taken back to her bed to change her soaked clothing, her stump throbbing mercilessly and the phantom pinging away. After a while, the pain began to subside, just as Miss Pembrey arrived to take a look at her; she expressed her unconcern, remarking that Hannah's collapse was probably due to nothing more than the effect of the excitement and effort on a body recovering from a serious invasion.Hannah pleaded to Frankie: 'Pleeeease don't tell anyone what happened in there. It'll only worry them.'

# 4

## Tilly Barker

**H**annah lay in bed and opened her eyes to see a girl looking at her at eye level; then: 'Hello … Umm … Hannah. And how are you today?' said the girl. 'I'm Tilly, short for Matilda. People usually want to know.'

Hannah looked at her sleepily: Tilly looked only three feet tall … no, she must be in a wheelchair. 'And how do you know my name?' she asked.

'I'm a patient, from that bed over there,' said Tilly. 'I see your consultant is Miss Pembrey, same as mine. And your name's there on the wall. Why are you here, anyway? … [Tilly looked at the contours of the light covering on Hannah's bed] … Oh, I see. How is it?'

'Aching like hell,' said Hannah. 'So what brings *you* here?'

'Thought I'd come over and see you – helps to pass the time, you know.'

'No, I mean why are you in ozzy?'

'Ah! Complicated. Are you sure you want to know?'

'Well, I don't know until you tell me.'

'Right. I was born with something called – wait for it – Proximal Focal Femoral Deficiency. Not many people have heard of it – it's quite rare – there's only something like one of us in a million. It's just that your leg bones grow in a wonky fashion. The bones of my left leg have never grown to match those of my right one, so it's always been too short. And I've had all sorts of surgery and stuff to try and put things right – to try and even my legs up. But what happened to *your* leg?'

'I was run over by a lorry. Time's a bit … wobbly in my head. The main problem I'm experiencing at the moment is that my

53

boyfriend hasn't been to see me … yet. My mum and little sis come regularly, and my big sis occasionally, but I don't think Tom likes the idea of a girlfriend with one leg. He was with me when the accident happened, and he came into ozzy in the ambulance with me, and that was it. I haven't seen him since. Nothing I can do about it. No point in calling him – it'll be even more awkward for him if I'm chasing him and he can't hack it.'

She realised how easy it was to talk to a stranger about Tom. She hadn't said any of this to her family.

'I'm sure it'll all get sorted in the end.'

'Umm … That's very reassuring of you. I can only wait and see … [How can I put this politely?] … I see you're in a wheelchair …?'

'Yes. Because at long last I've got rid of my wonky leg. I should've done something drastic about it ages ago, but they kept trying to put it right, and I kept believing that they'd be able to. It's such a long story … Hi mum. Just telling Hannah here about my wonky leg.'

'Surely she won't want to know about that, will she?'

'But I really am interested,' said Hannah. 'Please do tell me all about it. Helps to pass the time, you know,' she added mischievously.

'That's true,' laughed Bev, Tilly's mum. 'So Tilly's told you about the PFFD she's been dealt, has she?'

'Yes, but I'm still not really sure *exactly* what it is.'

'Ah! Wait for it … Proximal Focal Femoral Deficiency. What it means is that the bones of a leg are not 'normal', and were put together wrong in the womb and grow in a different way from those of a 'normal' leg. Very occasionally, both legs are wonky. When Tilly was born the doctor saw that something was wrong – but whatever it was, it hadn't shown up properly on the scans beforehand, which was a bit of a bag of rusty spanners.'

Tilly had heard the story many times before, but didn't mind her mum going through it all again.

'So almost from when Tilly was born, we were taking her off to one specialist leg clinic or another. There didn't seem to be any general agreement about treatment. Then, when she was about three years old, the consultant we were dealing with decided to fit her up with what's called an external fixator. They break the bone in the wonky leg on purpose, fasten this fixator thing to the broken ends of the bone, and then adjust it little by little, day by day, so that the bits of the broken-on-purpose leg bone are pulled apart, which is supposed to encourage the bone between to grow longer – they hoped. Sorry, are you happy with all this?'

'I'm fine. Carry on. And *did* the bone grow longer?'

'Not really. We had to turn the fixator adjusting screws bit by bit, day after day, but nothing much seemed to happen except pain. Over the years poor Tilly spent months with the fixator, and sometimes with her leg in plaster, and usually with a specially built-up shoe for her left leg, and crutches to help her walk, and a wheelchair as well, and weeks and weeks waiting for operations to happen, and then more weeks recovering from them.'

'It wasn't a happy childhood legwise,' chipped in Tilly. 'And then not too long ago they suggested a further series of operations that they thought might or might not work, and at that point I decided I'd had enough.'

'Phew! That must have been quite something. What did you do?'

'I researched on the internet and then asked Miss Pembrey to fuse my knee so that the two bits of bone on each side of it would together be long enough to make a femur, and then cut off the foot at the wonky end of the leg, but save the heel pad which is strong, and attach it to the end of the new femur to provide a weight-bearing stump, so that when it was ready I could be fitted with an all-singing, all-dancing prosthesis – an artificial leg.'

Hannah was realising that the longer she stayed in hospital, the more interested she became in medical details that she would have overlooked or found gruesome before.

Tilly continued: 'Before Miss Pembrey would do anything, she did loads more tests on my leg and lots of research into what might happen, but eventually she fused my knee, and then last week she amputated my foot except for my heel, and here I am waiting for the new bit that's left to heal so that I can have the wonderful prosthesis.'

'And how is it?' asked Hannah.

'Early days, and it feels as if it's being stabbed by monsters with huge knives,' said Tilly. 'But it does seem promising, I must say. Give it a week or two, and I'll be rarin' to go.'

'That must be a relief,' said Hannah. 'Couldn't they have done what they've just done ages ago?' Before her accident, she would never have had a conversation like this.

'Er ... well ... different wonky legs appear to need different treatments, and different surgeons have different ideas of what's best. I know that Miss Pembrey had to do a lot of research before agreeing to what I wanted. But I think they're a lot better at sorting out wonky legs nowadays than they used to be,' said Tilly. 'They get to grips with what to do earlier in a kid's life than they used to. 'Frinst, they didn't do anything at all for me till I was three years old. Nowadays, they might decide to do something when you're only a month or two old. Trouble is, think of your dilemma if you're a proud, protective, new parent and a surgeon suggests that amputating a perfect-looking little foot even if it's on the end of a wonky leg would be the best way forward, what then?'

'I can see that everything would be so unfamiliar that I might have no idea what course of action to choose ...'

'I used to sit on the sidelines and watch the other kids leading normal lives and doing sporty things, while I couldn't do any of that, and they called me things like stumposaurus, crippopotamus and worse. And then after all those operations, and with the prospect of many more ahead, and no guarantee of success anyway, I looked at shedloads of information on the web, and a light bulb came on in my head and I asked why I couldn't just have my knee fused and my foot amputated. And at last that's what's happening.'

'Double wow!' said Hannah, glad of an opportunity to get a word in. 'So, what's going to happen to you next?' She'd never come across a story like this before.

'Well, now I'm in this chair, or going around on crutches, until my newly-fashioned residual limb has healed enough for me to be fitted with a fake leg. Oddly enough, I feel more normal like this, as an amputee, than I did going about with one leg shorter than the other, and whatever was needed – a built-up shoe or whatever – to even me up.'

'I suppose so,' said Hannah. 'I guess all those bits and pieces you mentioned fastened on to you must have looked a bit odd, especially to people who weren't used to seeing such things.'

'Yes. But hang on,' said Tilly. 'I've been thinking about this. Kids must have been born into the world with wonky legs right back to the beginning of time. I was reading about it only last week. If you had a short leg not that long ago, you could have a special built-up shoe according to how much extra height the short leg needed, or you could have some other sort of leg extension, or just a pair of crutches while the leg hung free. In fact, some people nowadays use these devices – especially in more … er … backward places. People don't all want to be subjected to the modern fetish of trying to make them look "normal". And of course there are places where there's nobody to whom "normality" means anything, either physiologically or surgically.

'And the article went on to say that it's even possible to have your ankle moved up and turned round and made into a knee. Rotationplasty it's called. There's no end to what they can do – or at least try.'

'Umm. But if it's going to make you better, able to walk properly, it must be worth it.'

'Well … what's *better*? What's *properly*? We could talk about that all day.'

'Sure thing,' said Tilly's mum. 'But I've got to go and do some shopping now.'

'OK mum,' said Tilly. She turned towards Hannah. 'Are you off to the gym, or shall we go down to the canteen together?'

'I'm off to the gym now, and then I'll join you in the canteen, if that's OK,' said Hannah.

'OK,' said Tilly, 'Off I go in my wheelchair.'

Hannah snorted: 'I really hate using a wheelchair – it makes me feel sooo disabled. Like that blue disabled sign they have.' Grabbing her crutches, she set off for the gym, her mind full of wonky legs.

# 5

## Lucy Morgan

tall girl in a floral dress led Jill to the Relatives' Room with its comfortable but threadbare chairs: 'Mrs Brooks? I'm Lucy Morgan, psychological therapist ...'

'Yes?'

'Would you like a cup of coffee? Or tea? If you have a moment ...'

Lucy busied herself with making drinks while Jill admired the fluff on the dried flowers that – like everything else in the room – had seen better days. She had a sudden thought that if the hospital played its cards right she might fund a refurbishment of this Relatives' Room as a 'thank-you' when Hannah was released.

Lucy sat down: 'Well, Mrs Brooks ...'

'Yes ...?'

'I wouldn't blame you if you're having a bit of difficulty getting your head round what's happened to Hannah.'

'It was rather ... sudden ... harrowing ... and now I don't know what to think. It's a lot to take in.'

'It certainly is, but I'm here to help you. I know that families often find themselves under tremendous strain when something like this happens. It's so completely unexpected, isn't it? One minute whoever it is is off out somewhere, cheerily waving good-bye, and the next minute you hear they've had an accident and they won't be back today. Or perhaps ever. A huge shock. Everyone's whole world turns inside out. Upside down. Perhaps you could tell me a bit about Hannah? And your family set-up?'

'Well ... there's me and my husband Martin – who's not around very much – he's working on an engineering contract in the States – and our three daughters – the youngest Frankie, then Hannah, and Olivia's the eldest sister ... Hannah is ... *was* ... very active. Swimming is ... was her sport. She's good with her hands, too ... makes models with her sisters. Stage sets. She's pretty outgoing. Gets on with everybody. And she's done maths, chemistry and physics A-levels. She was just setting out to enjoy a gap year when *this* happened. Oh lordy, makes her sound too good to be true ...'

'Just an active, intelligent teenager – young adult. And she'll feel as if a great brake has been put on her activities. It'll be hard for her. Very hard. But I can assure you that with a positive approach she'll be able to get back to doing almost everything she did before. A bit more slowly, perhaps, but if she puts her mind to it ... and she may go through a whole range of emotions following her loss ... and so may you, and so may other members of your family. You have to be ready for that, and try to understand ...'

'I suppose it's a bit like when somebody dies ...?'

'It can seem very like that. A person has gone. And gone for ever. You'll never see them – talk to them – again. Ever. And just as you have to get on with living without the person who's died, so the amputee has to get used to living without the limb. And everyone has to get used to the amputee. But it's not easy ...'

There was that word ... 'amputee' ... Jill tried to continue without showing how much it still affected her.

'No, I can see that. Not easy for Hannah, not easy for us. But ...'

'Tell me a bit about your home set-up.'

'Yes ... we live at Victoria House ... [makes it sound as though everyone should know where that is] ... in Frimley ... we've lived there nearly twenty years. Moved just after Olivia was born. Lucky it had a stairlift left by the previous owners. That came into its own when Frankie broke her leg a couple of years ago. And it'll be doubly useful now ...'

'And how's the family taking Hannah's loss?'

'Interesting question. Frankie's very concerned of course but she's still in rather a daze. But she's so ... sensible; motherly, even towards Hannah. Olivia's an archaeologist, and she's away a lot of the time, but she's deeply concerned, of course … My husband Martin is also deeply concerned, but he's away in the States on business and we're a bit … separate at the moment. I'm trying to get used to what's happened; I'm finding it hard to get used to seeing Hannah with one leg. But I'm afraid Hannah's boyfriend Tom just doesn't seem to be able to accept what's happened. He accompanied Hannah here to A&E in the ambulance after the accident, but we haven't seen him since that evening. We're still waiting to see what happens.'

'Yes. I must warn you – it *could* happen that Tom'll *never* get over Hannah's loss. Sometimes the loss of a limb is just too much for someone close to the amputee to come to terms with. You can understand it if a friend or a partner finds the loss hard to take. More than one of my married patients has said that the divorce forced upon them following the accident was far worse than losing the limb. But it's early days … I'm sure the Victoria House set-up is very … supportive.'

'I think we can cope. But guidance is … will always be … welcome. We're … new to all this, of course. Except that, as I say, Frankie did break her leg a couple of years ago … So we know a bit about people getting around the house on crutches – looking out for obstacles and so on.'

'Well, we're here as long as you want us. But *we* need *your* help as well – we're used to this sort of situation, so we'll leave you to get on with it if you can – but we need to be reminded if we look … seem to be … too … complacent.'

'You mean we should come and talk to you if we need to?'

'Yes. I think it's very important that you should be able to turn to me if you think I can help. After all, I've had a fair amount of experience of this sort of disruption of the family.'

'Yes,' said Jill, not sure whether another meeting would be useful, but realising it would be wise to keep that as an option.

'And you need to be prepared to support whatever emotional roller-coaster Hannah finds herself riding. There are different ways of reacting, just as when someone dies. Hannah may now see herself as "incomplete" but a positive acceptance of her new self is crucial to her emotional recovery. There are said to be a number of stages to emotional recovery, though not everyone goes through them all in a set order, and trying to identify or document them – and failing – can lead to trouble. So I don't usually say anything about them, otherwise people may concentrate too hard on trying to identify them.'

'I think Hannah is very level-headed, and knows the score.'

'I'm sure she is and does. But it is possible that she'll experience shock, denial, anger and depression before she reaches acceptance, interwoven with despair, depression and withdrawal. You may find this booklet will help.'

'Thank you,' said Jill. ' And I'm sure it'll be helpful to have a chat in a week or two.'

Hannah looked up to see a new visitor, someone she had not met before: 'Hello, Hannah, I'm Lucy Morgan – psychological therapist. I've just been talking to your mum so I thought I'd pop along to see how you're getting on.'

'Very nice of you. I'm fine thanks … are you a … visitor?'

'Yes … if you have any doubts or worries, I'm here to help.'

'Oh! … Oh? What sort of doubts or worries?'

'Well … you've become an amputee …'

'People keep telling me that …'

'… so you may feel angry, or worried, or sad …'

'I don't feel any of that. The only thing that might help is turning the clock back … can you do that for me? NO! *I* can't, and *you* can't … and Stephen Hawking can't. But none of this makes me feel sad, or worried, or angry.'

'Ah! But suppose … do you not sometimes feel it's all too much?'

'No … [yes, but I'm not going to admit that to *you*] … but I spose there's always a first time. I do think that lots of people spend lots of time trying to alter things that can't be altered … trying to explain things that are inexplicable … trying to solve problems that are insoluble … and, of course, telling other people what they ought to be thinking, or feeling or doing … [ouch!]'

'I can see you've thought about it quite deeply … very deeply. Tell me, do you have many … outside interests?'

'Outside what? Well, I don't have too many *in*side … apart from watching the clock, and eating, and reading and sleeping, and physio, and getting used to … but yes. Swimming, diving, but I can't do those now … art & design, mathematics, puzzles … is that enough?'

'Wow! More than … How do you fit them all in?'

'Well … they're a part of life, really. Swimming and diving … but I can't do those now … no more of them at the moment … art & design – and handing over the running of a Maths Club …'

'You must be very organised.'

'Not really.'

'And do you think about it all in here?'

'Sometimes. I think about when I would be going swimming and diving, and how I'm going to be able to get up to the diving boards when I get out of here …'

'Ah! Will you be able to keep up with that … those?'

'Yes, if I can. I haven't worked it out yet. Except I used to go to the Golden Splash with my boyfriend Tom: in fact, we were on the way there when I had my accident. He came in to ozzy with me that day, but he hasn't been to see me since.'

'I'm sorry, but it's not unknown for someone close to a new amputee to disappear from the scene.'

'I suppose that's the way it is sometimes. Like now ...'

'Er ... What about ... mathematics?'

'I can do that sitting down.'

'Of course, but I just wondered what mathematics entails. What do you like about it particularly?'

'I find it all interesting ... but I'm particularly into geometry, Euclidean and co-ordinate, solid, topology ... part of the art & design thing ... and puzzles ... Sudoku ...'

'Yeah. What *about* the art & design thing?'

'Frankie – she's my little sister and Olivia – she's my big sister – we're all into making models of one sort or another. We design and make models of stage sets. You ought to see our rooms ...'

'I can imagine. To change the subject, would you mind if I send someone to see you who can talk to you about prostheses.'

Is that what she's been leading up to?

'At this point?'

Does she think that would be good for me then?

'Why not? While you're ... er ... coming to terms ... getting used to ...'

'You reckon? There seems to be such a lot of stuff to get used to here.'

'Never a dull moment in hospital. Anyway ... have a think about it ... we can chat again later. You need to take it easy.'

[Maybe I won't have to talk about prostheses yet then.]

'Okely dokely. It was really nice talking to you ... Please come again.'

'I will ... look after yourself, Hannah.'

ೋ

'Good day Honey. How are you doing? Been up to much today?'

'Hey mum ... Good to see you. Dolores's had me working out this morning!'

'Oh really … what's she got you doing this time?'

'More practice with balls … hard work though … And then there's wheelchair practise. And then the gym, which is a bit of a challenge …'

'I bet it is. You're just going to have to take your time. Take it easy. Y'know the usual phrases, *one step at a time* and all that.'

'Yes. I'm deffo gonna take it easy. Not like I'm in a great rush to get anywhere!'

'Precisely. Don't suppose they've washed your hair recently have they?'

'No … really need a shower … feel *awful* to be honest … but the closest I can get to that at the moment is a bed bath.'

'Yes … fraid that's the way at the moment. Mustn't get your dressing wet … you've got to wait until the wound's more healed before you can go getting into any showers or baths.'

'Yeah, that's how it is.'

'Well … how about I give your hair a wash … that should make you feel a lot better.'

'Yes … that'd be great. Thanks.'

'I'll go and have a word with one of the nurses; I'm sure it'll be fine with them.'

So Jill tracked down a nurse and asked her where she could give Hannah a clean-up; the nurse pointed to a room a little way down the corridor. Jill returned to Hannah, and helped her wheel to the bathroom and washed her hair, and her leg, and generally cleaned her up as best she could, trying to make her feel more comfortable and fresh, before returning her back to her bed.

'Here … I got these the other day …' Jill handed Hannah a little bag with drawstrings containing a few pots of make-up, some foundation, a small pot of eyeshadow, and an eyeliner pencil: 'Thought they might help cheer you up – rather than sitting here feeling crappy and messy. If you make yourself look nice, you'll feel better about yourself – *and* I've got you some face wipes. And a mirror …'

'Ah, thanks mum, that's great.'

'Ooo … Two more things … Got an appointment at Vicky at two … Vanessa Telford from the *Frimley Chronicle* wants to come and write an article about your accident. She hinted that you might want to raise funds to buy a prosthetic leg, and that they might be able to help. I thought you wouldn't mind so I gave her the go-ahead. You *don't* mind do you?'

'Well, it was *my* accident – so long as they don't go printing too much personal stuff … I'd like to have a private life when I get out of here … losing a leg'll get enough attention, but I don't want to be the one that everyone points at and makes comments like "Poor Lamb, Bless her cotton socks … sock … If only this … If only that." … I've got to live with it. They haven't. Sorry, I don't know how much sense that makes …'

'No worries Hun, I totally understand you. And you know I wouldn't go saying anything I shouldn't.'

'I know … where's Frank by the way?'

'She's gone into town. Sends you her love.'

'Cool, give her mine will you?'

'Of course … Well. I'll be off for now.'

Hannah winked at her mum, who kissed her on the forehead, said her goodbyes and left for Victoria House.

⁂

Martin was on his way to pay a surprise visit to Hannah in Kitty's – up to Hyacinth Ward and to the nurses' desk: 'Martin Brooks; I've come to see my daughter Hannah? … [Damn! I didn't mean to go up at the end] … She's …'

'Yes Mr Brooks. Hannah's through there in the room to the left and on the left.'

Martin entered the ward … left … left … and there was Hannah, sitting in her wheelchair, her left leg very missing; it gave him quite a start – he felt as though he'd been punched in the stomach to see Hannah – whom he'd never let on was his favourite daughter – in her new state.

Hannah saw her dad, forgot who and where she was, and made to leap up to greet him. Martin saw what was about to happen, and caught Hannah in his arms before she could fall. He kissed her on the forehead: 'Hello, Han … I was *so* sorry to hear about your accident. I came as soon as I could.'

'Dad … I'm *sooo* glad to see you. I had no idea you were coming. Have you had a good trip?'

'I sure have, and I've got … but that'll wait – how are you? I was so … shocked to hear what had happened … I'm so … sorry … [it seems inadequate] … to see you like this.'

'Well, this is how I am now, dad. The new me. You'll have to get used to it, like everybody else. Especially me.'

'Yes … well … are you in any pain?'

'Not too bad, now. The phantom limb – you know about that? – it can make me feel as if I've still got two legs, … except that the left one feels … a funny shape; with especially knotted toes. They warn you about forgetting you've only got one leg and stepping out and falling over. I haven't done that yet. But I nearly did just now – lucky you were there. And I'm not in a lot of pain … much less than you might think. They're very good at controlling pain. And I've been out of bed a few days now, and I started by using the walking frame, and I scooted about in this chair, as Dolores will say, and started walking on crutches … although I still have to adjust for the loss of weight on my left side and the way my balance has changed.'

'Well … what happens next?'

'I'll be in here a few days yet; physio and more physio; then when they take the stitches out I should be home soon after that.'

'The stitches …?'

'Yes … I've got 47 stitches round here. [Hannah indicated the line.] Don't forget that legs don't just snap off cleanly and tidily; they have to tidy up what's left and sew you together.'

'I suppose they do. How much leg have you left? And how long will you have to wait for a new leg?'

'Well, they can't do much until the stump's healed and settled down … a month or three, I think. But I'm going to wait and see … I'm told not to forget that a wheelchair is a form of prosthesis. But I must say that I'd far rather use my crutches. And they won't let me out of here until someone from OT – occupational therapy – has been round the house and passed it as OK for people with missing legs'

'Ah …'

Hannah had realised that going to the loo could be a subtle way of getting people used to seeing her in action. As she set off, Martin observed her neat and increasingly practised manoeuvre; seeing her one-leggedness properly for the first time, he felt that lump in his throat again, and all manner of thoughts about what had happened to his daughter and the effect it had had – and would have – on her – on everybody – raced through his mind: anger, sadness, frustration. He sat as if in a trance. Soon, Hannah returned, sat down, and smoothed her skirt in what was becoming an automatic movement. She gave a little wriggle and burst into tears: 'Oh! I'm so sorry …'

'What's the matter, My Han?'

'Oh! Sorreee … That's just one of the things you have to get used to …'

'What?'

'You can't use one foot to push your slipper off the other. So you have to use some other method. Such as the end of a crutch.'

'I expect there're all sorts of things like that …'

'Yes, and they suddenly leap out and remind you what's

happened to you. Some they warn you about. Others you have to find out … for yourself. Don't suppose it ever ends … So, how's work going? Are you staying here for a bit?'

Martin avoided the latter question and they turned to his work and chatted until the evening meal came round, and he took this as his cue to leave. He gave Hannah a hug and kissed her on the forehead. She looked into his eyes and saw a look of sad bewilderment. She knew her accident was all rather too much for the jet-lagged Martin to be dealing with – or for *anyone* to be dealing with for that matter, especially her.

'I hope you know how proud I am of you,' he said. 'Of how you're doing. How you're coping with all this.'

'I have to, I've *got* to, if I want to carry on with my life. I can't stop just like that – see, that's the thing?'

'Yes. I suppose it is. I'm glad you've such a good head on those shoulders. You're going to do well. I'll certainly do what I can to help you.'

'Thanks Pa. Love to everybody. Take care.'

'Cheers, and you make sure you get plenty of rest. And concentrate on getting yourself fit and healthy …'

'Hey!'

'What?'

'I *am* fit, and I *am* healthy. I'm here for the physio and rehab. And I want home asap.'

'Sorry, Han. I'll remember … see you …'

※

With that, Martin left. Hannah sat and tucked into her dinner, thinking about a conversation she'd once had, about how you feel your brain is inside your cranium … is that because you know it's there, or because you can really feel yourself thinking there? Now that she was concentrating so much on her stump, she suddenly felt that her brain had moved there, and when she closed her eyes she had a vivid stump's-eye-view of her body. And her left leg was rolled up tightly inside. Weird!!! Her thoughts turned into a dream, and she was asleep.

Martin made his way home to Victoria House, where Jill was preparing the evening meal. It was the first time they had all (apart from Hannah) been at home since the accident the previous Friday, and Jill was glad that everyone would be sitting down together. She called the girls.

Somewhat tentatively, Martin took his place at the head of the table. Frankie went to the kitchen to fetch the vegetables, and Jill brought in the lasagne: 'Glad we can all eat together tonight.'

'But without Han ...'

'Yes Olly, sorry, without Han. Think we could also do with a chat about how things around here might have to change. About how we're going to deal with this.'

'And there's something I need to say too,' said Martin.

Jill thought she knew what that might be: 'Perhaps that'd be a good place to start,' she said. She began to serve the meal, wondering how Martin would proceed.

'I'm sure you've noticed I've been away quite a bit recently,' began Martin.

'We've sort of ... got used to it,' said Olivia.

'And we've got a sort of ... impression that you're a bit ... tired of us,' said Frankie.

There was a silence.

'I'm here recharging my batteries,' said Martin.

Jill wondered whether to make things easier for him. If things had to be like this, they were very lucky to be able to live in harmony and without fighting.

'I suppose you've got a lot going on over there,' she said. 'As well as work ...?'

'Not really,' said Martin, avoiding the opening. 'I'm up to my ears in the job. But it is going very well. But I must say I'm devastated by Han's accident, although I think she's doing *ama*zingly well considering; she's up and walking around on crutches almost as if she was ... born to it.'

'Yes ... she's really good at getting about. There's not much stuff, like physically, that we've gotta change around here, is there?'

'No, you're right, it's all pretty well sorted now.'

'Ah ... that's something Han mentioned to me ... she said we should be expecting an occupational therapist to come visiting – the key person that decides if the house is safe enough for Hannah to live in.'

'Yes. We've got to make sure that everything's perfect. We want our Han to be able to come home just as soon as she can. The quicker she's out of that ozzy place, the better.'

'I agree. Tell you what – tomorrow, let's walk round the house – and the garden – slowly, and look for hazards – trippy cables, loose mats, all that sort of thing.'

'Good idea.'

Jill thought about Hannah's homecoming: 'Mainly though ... it's our attitudes ... that's what we've got to watch.'

'Yes mum,' said Frank '... I agree ... and this concerns us all. We can be ready to help Han as much as she wants us to, but we must *never* appear to be taking over. She's going to want to do stuff by herself ... gotta be able to ... yknow, be self sufficient, just like she would if she were normal ... well, had two legs. Or were living alone.'

Olivia thought about this: 'Yeah ... that may take some getting used to,' she said. 'I guess we'll have to keep an eye on all the things that happen, and learn when we're needed.'

'And when we're not needed,' said Frankie.

Yeah … Han'll want to fend for herself; we must respect that. But we must also be ready when our help's *really* needed, however stubborn she is, wanting to do stuff for herself.'

'And we have to be upfront; not beat about the bush. Otherwise, we'll spend a lot of time skirting round a subject, and the demon amputation will have won.'

'How do you mean …?'

'Well, as I see it, it would be so easy for Han's O-L-ness to take over as the most important thing about her. And the most important thing in all our lives.'

'Yes,' said Martin. 'We've got to look forward, not back. There's absolutely no reason why Han's new shape should take us over. There's nothing we – anyone – can do to change things, so we have to get on with it. D'you see …?'

'Ye-e-es … anyway …'

'I'm glad we can all talk about this,' said Frankie. 'It'll make it so much easier for Han – and for us – if we can …'

'Do you think we ought to have a homecoming party for Han?' asked Olivia. 'Just for our close friends, and especially those who haven't seen her since … the accident.'

'That could be a good idea,' said Frankie. 'Obviously we don't want it to be too … serious, but we could let Han explain what's happened to her. Not sure if we should ask Han about it, or arrange it for a surprise …'

And with that thought, the room fell silent. Frankie made coffee for everyone and they moved outside to the terrace. They sat quietly as the sun went down, each with their own thoughts. Frankie imagined O-L-er Hannah sitting out on the terrace with them – as no doubt she would be in a week or two. The picture became more than she could bear and, concealing her tears, she kissed everyone goodnight and went off to her room.

# 6
## Meg Brown

rankie came into Hyacinth Ward after breakfast: 'Have a look at this bit from the *Chronicle*,' she said, passing Hannah a cutting:

# Lorry crushes teen's leg: cyclist's horrific accident

*Our special reporter Vanessa Telford*

A Frimley girl was seriously injured last Friday morning when she was run over by a lorry on the Tamthorpe Road while cycling to the Golden Splash Swimming Pool. The victim, who has not been named but is believed to be a local teenager, became trapped at the Chequers Roundabout on the Tamthorpe Road and her leg was crushed by the lorry.

The girl was taken to St James's hospital, where her injuries were said to be 'serious, but not life-threatening'.

A spokeswoman said that police were trying to trace the lorry, which is believed to have a large letter "E" and a butterfly painted on it. Members of the public who have any information are asked to contact Sgt Julie Templeton on Frimley 372737.

'Reckon that bit in the *Chronicle* must've alerted a few people to your … accident. Here's another bunch of cards and things. And an important-looking letter – from *3–6–9 Productions*, whoever they may be …'

Hannah took the post: 'Thanks, Frankie …'

She opened the cards, saving *3–6–9 Productions* till last: 'Here goes … Ohmigod …'

'What?'

'Some production company wanting to get in touch.'

> *Dear Miss Brooks,*
> *We were very sorry to read in the* Frimley Chronicle *about your accident …* [there, I knew it, thought Hannah] *… and sincerely hope that you're making a good recovery. However, every cloud has its silver lining, and I'm wondering if you might be able to assist us with a hospital documentary we are making about young people recovering from serious accidents. Without wishing to be intrusive, I hope you will be willing to have a chat with one of our researchers who will be pleased to tell you more about the project and answer any questions you may have.*
> *Kind regards*
> *Hilary Faith*
> *3–6–9 Productions*

Hannah passed the letter to Frankie, who studied it carefully: 'Oh, Han. That's exciting, but how do we know it's *bona fide*? It could be from anyone. It makes me feel … I know I'm being suspicious – paranoid, even – you never can tell …'

Frankie got out some paper and started to scribble. At last: 'How's this, Han? …'

*Dear Ms Faith*
*Thank you for your letter addressed to Miss Brooks.*
*We would be grateful if you would send details of your*
*company, and information about the programmes you*
*make and the fees you pay for the various activities*
*in which Miss Brooks might be involved, such as*
*giving specialist advice, taking part in interviews, or*
*appearing in your productions. Please reply to me at*
*Victoria House, as Miss Brooks is likely to be out of*
*action for some time yet.*
*Yours sincerely*
*Frances Brooks*
*Co-ordinator*


'There!'

'Frank ... that's masterly – how did you think of all that? Let's have a look ... umm ... what sort of co-ordinator are you? Rehab, perhaps?'

'Yeah, could be. Or perhaps *Ms H Brooks's personal assistant. Personal assistant to Ms H Brooks* ... How's that?'

'Great. Who can we try it out on? What about Lucy Morgan? Let's see what happens with her first. If we don't reply to her straight away, maybe Hilary Faith will write again ... So, how're things at home?'


Frankie didn't stay long, so after lunch, Hannah went off to the Day Room with some puzzles to help pass the time. Just as she was grappling with a Sudoku, a largish woman with a big smile approached her: 'Hello, you must be Hannah ...'

'Umm ... yes ...?'

'I'm Meg Brown ... I'd like to talk about your leg. Can we go somewhere quiet?'

'It's quiet here, isn't it? What *about* my leg. Which one?'

'Er ... both of them, I suppose ... Lucy Morgan suggested ... [she would, thought Hannah] ... she said I might be able to help you see the way forward. One of the nurses said that you'd be in here. I'm not interrupting you, am I?'

'Oh no, that's fine. But how do you think you can help me?'

'Well, as I understand it, you've lost your left leg above the knee ...'

'Umm. Yes ...?'

'Well ... so have I, and Lucy thought it might help you if I explained what can be done ... showed you what my leg is like ...'

'And what *is it like*? Are you and Lucy going to *make* me look like you?'

'Haha. Not exactly ...'

As Meg showed Hannah her prosthesis, and explained how it was constructed, and how it was attached to her, and how it worked, Hannah started to come round to Meg's idea of 'getting fixed up', as they would put it.

She also decided that as Meg was quite easy to talk to, she might as well ask her a few questions: 'Well, thanks ... umm ... I've just seen your wedding ring.'

'Yes?'

'And did you meet your husband ... er ... before or *after* ...?'

'After. Are you worried you might not find anyone?'

'Well ... no ... but ... Where'd you meet him?'

'At a disco. Some friends thought I needed cheering up. Actually, I didn't, but I thought it could be fun. And we went to this hall, and Kevin and I immediately saw each other across the room – WHAM! – it was love at first sight. I can assure you that it can happen. It was quite crowded, so he worked his way over to me; then he saw my crutches, and stared a bit when he saw I only had one leg, but it seemed to make no difference to him after the initial surprise. We found ourselves talking about everything as if we'd been lifelong buddies. He did ask me about my leg, but he took it all … in his stride … so to speak. And he didn't tell me about someone he'd known who'd lost both arms and still become a top brain surgeon.'

'Some people want to tell you about an amputee who's capable of amazing feats, don't they? Sort of minimises what's happened to you.'

'Yes. You have no business to be inconvenienced.'

'Uhuh. When did … What happened to your leg … ?'

'I was fourteen, and playing football in the last match of the season. I lined up to take a penalty, and as I ran forward and kicked the ball there was a "crack" and the most excruciating pain in my leg. It turned out to have broken, but I *did* score that penalty and we *did* win the match, and that made the headlines! Anyway, I was carted off to A&E where they patched me up of course but then investigated the ease with which my leg had broken. And that was when they found a malignant tumour on my femur and decided that there was no alternative to amputation, followed by chemotherapy – and the sooner the better. I must say, I didn't get much – *hardly any* – advice or counselling … and no say in what was going to happen to me at all. No opportunity to discuss the treatment, or how to cope with becoming an amputee and feeling awful, and all my hair falling out. Of course, I could hardly have *not* agreed to the surgery, but it would've been nice to've been properly consulted and mentally prepared, as they say these days. And then afterwards they just gave me a pair of crutches and left me to get on with it, because they seemed to think I'd find it obvious how to use them. What happened to you? Lucy didn't say.'

'I was run over by a lorry, and lost my leg in the accident. Miss Pembrey tidied up what was left of the leg and built me this stump.'

'Ah, bad luck. But that's how it goes, sometimes … Anyway,

I met Kevin when I was twenty-one, and we were married two years later. I'm thirty-five now. And we've got a boy and a girl; Roland's nine, Bryony's eleven. They think mummy's leg's really interesting. But they know *never* to touch it when I'm not wearing it. I've never had any trouble being a mum. Or being *anything else*, if it comes to that. So your turn *will* come, and if I can be of any help …'

'Misjudged her at first,' thought Hannah, 'I can see Meg could be as much help as a lot of the others put together. Professional experience is one thing, but none of them has actually lost a leg.'

'Well … there are quite a lot of things you might be able to …'

'Try me …'

'They keep telling me I'm going to forget my leg's gone and take a step on it, but it's not there so I fall over. That's only happened once, I'm glad to say. What about *you*?'

'At the beginning it happened a couple or three times perhaps, but not for years now.'

'And what about pain? Or phantom feelings?'

'I'm glad to say they've got more and more rare as time goes on. I used to have sharp stabs in my stump from time to time, and my phantom foot would make its presence felt in the night, but that doesn't happen so much these days.'

'So there's hope for me … How much do you … umm … *wear* … your leg?'

'Good question. It's a much better leg now than when I first joined the club twenty-odd years ago. I started off using crutches or a wheelchair most of the time, as my first artificial leg was a bit of a challenge. A few legs later, I'm a lot more comfortable with it; I usually plan when I'm going to put it on and take it off – don it and doff it – depending on what I'm going to be doing. It's helpful when I go round the shops; carrying things; and at home as well – cleaning, cooking, laying the table, serving meals …'

'Do you use crutches much?'

'Dolores'll kill me for telling you this, but you ought to get yourself a pair of axillary crutches – old-fashioned ones that fit under your arms – they can be amazingly useful. They look as though you should rest your armpits on them, but you shouldn't – you squeeze them between your upper arm and your body, and take your weight on your hands. However, when you get good at it, you can move axillary crutches with just your upper arms, but then you *do* have to rest your armpits on them. But they can be adapted to walking in that way – in fact, one person I worked with had lost an arm above the elbow as well as a leg, but could still use an axillary crutch.

'I like walking with a single axillary crutch – like Long John Silver I suppose. You have to place the end of the crutch on the ground where your foot would be if it were still there. Then you pivot slightly on the crutch as you step your leg forward. That's how you can walk smoothly … it's not at all the same as walking on two crutches … with just one, you've got to try and use it as your missing leg and not as a crutch … if you see what I mean. And not to hop. Anyway, you'll find out for yourself. But I can show you if you like.'

'Wow! And yes … that would be good. As long as it isn't dangerous. Especially to *us*.'

'That's *another* thing. You have to realise how precious that leg you've still got is. Look after it and don't do anything … *silly*. Don't be tempted to walk barefoot.'

'Ah … good point … in fact I'm going to call my leg My Precious to remind me.'

'And the same with your crutches … sometimes people – especially young people – treat them as *toys*; wanting to "*have a go*". So they grab your crutches, and mess around with them. Your crutches are as valuable as your leg, so don't let them out of your sight.'

'Did that happen to you at school … with one leg?'

'Well, I was in a wheelchair for a lot of the time, but when I started using crutches a lot more, I had some very good friends who shielded me from … less sympathetic people. I got a prosthesis that I didn't like very much when I was in the sixth form, but I didn't have much trouble from other people then. Are you still at school?'

'No, I finished my A-levels last year and I'm having a year out. Mind you, losing a leg has upset my plans a bit, but at least I've got time to learn to be an O-L-er.'

'Good for you! Remember, you can do anything you set your mind to. It may take a little longer than it used to, but …'

'What clothes did you find easiest to wear at school? Well … at any time?'

'Ah … school uniform was skirt or trousers, but I only wore a skirt if it was very hot weather, as I'm not built like a fairy, and the leg that I have isn't my best feature. I wore trousers adapted to be one-legged most of the time.'

'What about swimming?'

'No problem; I use what's called a legsuit with legs long enough to hide my stump, and use the changing cubicle nearest to the pool, so I don't have to hop very far.'

'Have you come across … umm … stalkers?'

'Have I? They're one of the things you haven't bargained for. You'll see people pretend not to look at you, walk away and then suddenly seem to forget something and turn towards you again to have a surreptitious look. Sometimes they sprint round the block and then come towards you again. It's spooky at first; then it becomes mildly amusing and exasperating at the same time. Sometimes I say "hello". That flummoxes them … Sometimes they walk into lamp-posts and plate-glass windows …'

'Ah! And do you get … fan mail? Let me show you something …'

Hannah got out her 3–6–9 letter and Frankie's draft reply: 'What do you think … ?'

Meg read the correspondence: 'Yep. I'd be very surprised if it were genuine. Good reply. Who's Frankie?'

'My little sister. I have a big sister too, Olivia.'

'It's good to have a Frankie … or an Olivia … or both … especially in the early stages when you need support. I should send that letter off, and see what happens. *Nothing* is my guess.'

'Yeah. Well … we'll do that … and let you know. Thanks for all you've told me. Any other tips?'

'Hundreds, I should think, but we can talk again some time if you like. And don't hop … too much. Puts a strain on your good leg. Mind you; you're quite light, I should say?'

'Bit over 50 kg … now'

'The lighter you are, the less effort to move around. And when you get a leg, it's got to fit snugly. Any change in your shape can be disastrous …'

'What if you get pregnant?'

'Ah! Then you'll likely spend a lot of time on crutches, or in your chair. But I can assure you it's worth it. Having a family, I mean.'

'Umm …'

'There's a lot to learn in this business. A lot more even than they'll tell you. You'll keep coming across new … challenges. Now, I've got to go, but here's my contact details, and don't hesitate –'

'Thanks. I won't … and … you've done me a *power* of good. I'm *so* glad Lucy asked you to … *call in* …'

Hannah watched Meg walk out of sight.

'Wow! She walks really well for an O-L-er,' she thought.

# 7
## Rachel Dibbs

smiling, rotund figure appeared at Hannah's bedside: 'Hello … [she glanced at the notice by the bed] … Hannah, isn't it? I'm Rachel Dibbs, Vicar of … [surely not Dibley? thought Hannah] … Frimley. I'm – haha – wearing my hospital visiting hat.'

Hannah envisaged this imaginary headgear while firmly shaking Rachel's somewhat limply proffered hand; she thought she might as well be pleasant to her, even though she felt she didn't want to talk to a vicar.

'I see you've lost a leg,' said Rachel. 'Bad luck. When did that happen?'

Hannah bristled: 'Eleven days ago. I had an argument with a lorry.'

'Oh yes, I read about it in the *Chronicle*, didn't I? I do hope you're recovering – I must say you look very well …'

'Umm …' said Hannah, 'I look well because I'm not ill. I've lost a leg but otherwise I'm fit and rarin' to go.'

'Yes, I suppose so. I'm sure you're anxious to get a new leg. Is there anything – haha – I can do for you?'

'Well … you've got friends in high places; perhaps you could get my leg restored …?'

Rachel laughed nervously: 'Ah, well, you see, it doesn't work like that.'

Hannah smiled sweetly: 'Ah! … Well, then … how exactly *does* it work?'

'It depends what *it* is. But I can assure you that God is *always* at your side.'

'So I've heard. But why didn't He – or She – help me when I was about to be run over by a lorry?'

'Well, as I said, it doesn't work like that ...'

'And, as *I* said, how *does* it work?' Hannah was feeling tetchy, and couldn't help herself.

'Ah ... well ... God loves us all, and if you have what you think is an accident, you can be sure that it's part of His purpose.'

'Can I really? It's not very loving to shove one of your children under a lorry, now, is it? ... I should tell you that I'm *very* disappointed in God, and even more disappointed in people who tell me that what's happened to me is all part of His purpose. As far as I can see, living *without* God makes the way things are seem much more explicable and understandable ... things just happen. I set out for the Golden Splash early in the morning to go diving, and I was run over by a lorry and it relieved me of my leg ... [can I make her squirm? wondered Hannah] ... and then they brought me here and took me to the operating theatre and tidied up what was left of it ... [Hannah patted and smoothed the left hand side of her skirt ... Rachel looked somewhat uneasy] ... end of story. Quite straightforward. I can't see how that's all part of God's Great Plan.'

Hannah sank back into her pillows, glad to have got it all off her chest, proud of the way she had spoken so fluently, while so close to tears, and realising that she might have hurt Rachel. But Rachel just smiled and said 'Very good. But one day, Hannah ... [she's taking my name in vain] ... you may come to see the truth. I hope you will ... and if there's anything I can do meanwhile ... I'll look in on you again ... [I probably won't be here, with any luck] ... Bless you Hannah, and thank you for your time.'

⁊⌒

A woman in a sharp business suit appeared and made her way over to Hannah: 'I'm Georgia Miller ... I hope I'm not intruding

... Rachel! Fancy seeing you here!'

'Hardly a surprise,' said Rachel. 'I work here ... when I'm wearing my hospital visiting hat ... remember?'

'How can I help you?' asked Hannah, feeling somewhat left out.

'Well,' said Georgia, 'Rachel knows, but you may not – I'm a compensation lawyer, and I believe you may be able to claim some compensation as a result of your accident.'

'So God isn't all bad?'

'How do you mean?'

'Well Rachel here has just been trying to tell me that my accident was all part of God's purpose – except that it now seems that God has laid on the possibility of some compensation – which is very helpful of Him.'

'Have you been able to trace the lorry then?' asked Rachel.

'I've just come from interviewing Inspector Hutchinson at the police station; I heard all about the E-butterfly lorry that ran you down but, curiously, they haven't been able to trace it – yet. We'd like to be able to help you with funds to pay for various home comforts, not to mention a state-of-the-art prosthesis when the time comes. But we do have to get a bit closer to the cause of the accident.'

'First catch your lorry,' said Hannah. 'Presumably God is having a fine old game of cat and mouse – the good news is ... the bad news is ... I think we're better off without God. What do you want from me?'

'Well, basically, I wanted to meet you and see if you had any further information about your accident tucked away in the back of your mind.'

'I don't really remember anything about the accident. And as far as I know, only my boyfriend at the time, Tom Curtis, spotted the E-butterfly, and I haven't seen him since then.'

'Ah! I think I'd better go round and make some more enquiries.

Here's my card. Let me know if anything further comes to light.'

Rachel also left her card on Hannah's table, and when Hannah opened her eyes again, she was nowhere to be seen. Hannah felt better – but still she had a good cry.

And while she was crying, Frankie came into the ward; she stood uncertainly for a moment; then darted over to Hannah, took her in her arms and hugged her: 'Oh, Han … what's the matter … everything suddenly …?'

'Oh … I just had a visit from the Vicar of Dibley … no … it was Rachel Dibbs, Vicar of Frimley,' she laughed.

'And what happened?'

'Oh, Frank … you'd've been proud of me … she wanted to tell me that losing my leg was all part of God's Great Plan …'

'And you retaliated by telling her that you'd never heard so much …'

'Right. It was so silly … I really laid into the poor woman …'

'If she comes again …'

'A second coming?'

'… yeah … you can tell her …'

'… that I think my leg's starting to grow again? A miracle!'

'Cruel! Meanwhile … mum said you'd taken to wearing trousers with a dangling leg.'

'Yes, well, I tried it. It didn't get caught up with anything but today, you see, I'm trying a skirt. I want to try lots of different clothes.'

Frankie gave Hannah another hug; then picked up her bag.

Hannah looked at her sister: 'What's in that bag?'

'I've brought you some books and a new top that I think you'll like.'

'Cool!!! Let's have a look.'

# 8

## Ben Riley

It was a beautiful morning, and after an early gym session Hannah was out in the hospital grounds. Her dressing had been changed, and she was out on her crutches with her empty left trouser leg dangling. Suddenly, she realised that she'd walked quite a distance; she was tired, and wondered if perhaps she'd been a bit silly and exerted herself too much, so she found a bench next to a colourful flower-bed, and sat down gingerly, her stump throbbing. She parked her crutches carefully against the arm of the seat, but they promptly slid sideways and clattered to the ground. Once again, she was struck with the 'first time I've done this' thought. She arranged her left trouser leg hanging flatly over the edge of the seat, closed her eyes in the warm sunshine, and felt a little better.

A voice interrupted her reverie: 'Mind if I sit here?'

It was a boy about her age, Hannah guessed: 'Feel free …'

There was a long silence between them as the birds sang, the traffic rumbled, a JCB clanked in the distance and ambulance sirens came and went as a continual reminder that they were in hospital grounds.

At long last, they spoke at the same time: ' 'What … ?' '

'You first …'

'No, you …'

'I was going to say – what are you in here for?'

'Ah … I've had a lot of trouble with something called ulcerative colitis, so they've operated on my intestines and made an ileostomy for me.'

Even as he spoke, the boy was trying to compare the seriousness of his ileostomy with that of the girl's amputation.

'Oh, poor you. I don't know what that is … if you don't mind … ?'

Hannah had become used to talking about medical details.

'Of course not. If you're sure you want to know. They remove your colon and bring the end of your small intestine through a hole in the side of your tummy down here … so that stuff comes here instead of going through your colon and coming out at the … umm … *usual place.*'

'Wow! So why doesn't it …?'

'Er … You stick a bag over the hole. And when the bag gets full, you unstick it, and throw it away, and stick on another one. But I'm not going to show you. And don't tell *every*body … I only told *you*, because we're in hospital.'

'No. Yes. It's cool.' Hannah thought about ileostomies and bags full of stuff, and wondered what it all looked like. Ben wondered if he'd impressed her: 'So what happened to your leg?'

Hannah was beginning to get used to that question: 'A lorry knocked me off my bike and ran over it …'

'Oww! That's big time awful! Does it hurt … much?'

'On and off. They're pretty good at controlling pain here, but it does stab and throb from time to time. And I still get phantom feelings, which are when it feels as though the bit that's gone is still there. That's quite weird. Anyway, what's your name?'

'Ben. Ben Riley. And …?'

'Hannah. Hannah Brooks. I really hope I'll be out of here soon.'

'I hope I will, too. When did it happen?'

'Twelve days ago at about 6.30 in the morning. Hey!! … That sounds like I've been kind of reborn in a new shape, like a new mum calculating her new baby's age to the nearest hour. But, yes, it's amazing how quickly one mends. I'll be having the stitches out very soon.'

'Stitches? Oh … yes … Where?'

Hannah traced the line of her stitches on her trouser leg:

'Forty-nine of them ... round here. But I'm not going to show you ...'

'Wow! So what's it like ... having one leg?'

'Well ... it's ... how it is. You mustn't think you still have two, even if the phantom tells you that you have. If you forget you've only got one leg, you might try to take a step with the one that isn't there and fall over. And that can hurt like hell.'

'Wow! Have you done that?'

'Almost ... once. Luckily my dad was there to catch me. But they keep warning me there's always a first time ... [Hannah thought dispassionately about having one leg] ... Anyway, now that the leg's gone I feel much lighter on the left-hand side. Probably lost ten kilos or so. Quite a difference. My balance is all different. Still getting used to it.'

'Yeah. So are you getting an ... an artificial leg?'

'Umm ... I'll find out about that in due course as well. When I'm properly healed. It was only twelve days ago, y'know. Give us a chance ...'

'I'm majorly sorry ... so how long does it take to ... heal?'

'Well, the stitches come out any moment now, but of course the wound's still tender – it takes a few weeks to heal properly. And of course the bit left – they call it a stump – needs to be really strong to take the socket of a fake leg. But's'OK. I'm getting a bit tired now, I think I ought to go back to the ward.'

Hannah stood up and nearly lost her balance; she leant over and grasped the back of the seat, remembering her crutches were on the ground: 'Ben ...? D'you think you could do something for me ... pick up my crutches?'

'Yeah, sure ... here ...'

Ben picked up the crutches somewhat gingerly and put out a hand to steady Hannah as she took a little hop, grasped the crutches and composed herself: 'Thanks, Ben ...' She stepped off slowly and deliberately.

'Hey, you do that … really well … and the way your trouser leg hangs is quite a disguise …'

Hannah realised that Ben had never seen her walking on two legs – and never would. Come to that, he'd never seen her before. It gave her one of those 'before and after' feelings: 'Well, I've had to have a bit of practice …'

They walked slowly back to the hospital entrance and entered the main concourse. At the lift, Ben stood against the door to prevent it closing on Hannah as she crutched in: 'Where to?'

'Sycamore. And you?'

'Hyacinth. Same floor. Opposite wing.'

They stood in silence as the lift ascended. The doors opened, and they stepped out on to the landing.

'Hannah …?'

'Yep?'

'Can I come and see you … on the ward?'

'Of course … or maybe *I'll* come and see *you* … cos I might be going home … whenever.'

'Right …'

They smiled and parted. Each felt the common bond of people who meet for the first time in unusual circumstances. Back in her hospital room Hannah lay on her bed and reflected on her meeting with Ben, wondering what it would be like to find that one needed, and then to have, an ileostomy.

Then she looked down her nose at her trousers, and realised again that Ben had never seen her with two legs. For everybody she'd known before the accident, seeing her now with one leg would be something new to them. And for some reason she felt their attitude towards her might now be different – possibly embarrassed. Why? She had to be 'Hannah with one leg', not 'an amputee.' But from now on, no one she met anew would have ever seen her with two legs – a distressing thought. She realised that she was making heavy weather of all this, but saw that it was all part of accepting her condition without question. She'd have to, because that was how it was.

℘

The next day, as Hannah lay with her book resting on her leg, she thought about how trousers – or a long skirt – might help to disguise O-L-ness when you were standing up, but could enhance it when you were lying down. And she was still thinking about Ben. She decided to try her frilly blue denim skirt again.

℘

In Sycamore, Ben was lying on his bed thinking about Hannah, when his mother appeared with a selection of books: 'Hi, Ben, darling.'

'Mum! Good to see ya. And the books. Thanks.'

'Anything been happening since I last saw you?'

'Big time. Went to see the stoma nurse yesterday …'

'And what did she say?'

'That everything's going on OK. And I've got the routine for changing the bag, and various helpful wipes and cleaners, and I should be able to come home soon. I went for a walk later, and met a lovely girl on the way back, sitting on a seat in the garden.'

'Yes? She a patient, or what?'

'Big time. Lost a leg eleven, no, twelve days ago.'

'Wow! She was in a wheelchair?'

'No, *sitting on a seat in the garden*. The empty leg of her trousers dangling over the edge – at first I didn't realise she only had one leg. And she gets along fine on crutches. I'm going to see her again. Mum, she's really done something for me. What's having a stoma, compared to losing a leg?'

'Well … she made you feel better, then?'

'spose so.'

'I don't think you can compare these things. You had colitis and all that went with it for a long time, and now they've sorted it out surgically. She's ... what happened to her leg, by the way? Did you find out?'

'Yeah ... She fell under a lorry ...'

'Oh yes ... YES! Of course! I saw it in the paper. Just a little paragraph. I'll bring it in for you – if I can find it. If you'd like.'

'Thanks.'

'Yeah ... well ... so *you've* been sorted out surgically, but *she* was perfectly well but had an accident. So losing her leg wasn't to *cure* anything, like your stoma was.'

'Well, I still think a stoma's ...'

'Yes. Perhaps. But I still don't think you can compare.'

There was a clicking of crutches; Hannah had decided to visit Ben after Frankie had left her: 'Hi Ben ... I thought I'd come and visit you, if it's not ...'

Ben leapt up and pulled a chair round: 'Of course not ... Hannah ... meet my mum ...'

'Hello ... [Help! Meeting his mum already. Better get her name right. You can never be sure – hope the name on the wall's right] ... Mrs Riley ...?'

'Hello Hannah. Glad to meet you. I gather you're quite a hero ... heroine ...'

'No. Not at all. And I'm not brave, or plucky, or any of those things ... in the paper my leg got tangled with a lorry – well, actually, the lorry got tangled with my left leg – and now I'm an O-L-er – someone with one leg. Oh ... sorry to go on, but ...'

'Yes, I know what you mean. It's the way the media deal with these things. They need a 'human story', so you have to be plucky, or brave. To you, it was a sequence of events. And all the while you were the same person.'

'Wow! That's so true ... I've been thinking about that, and now you've ...'

'Why don't you sit down?'

Hannah manoeuvred herself to the chair as a familiar clank heralded the tea-trolley. Once they had all had tea and biscuits Mrs Riley was unstoppable: 'Tell me, Hannah, you live in that big house on Victoria Road don't you? I've often wondered what goes on there.'

'My dad's an engineer; he runs his business there when he's not abroad – designs things – but he spends more and more time in the States. And my mum writes her novels there …'

'Jill Brooks! Yes … I think I've read most … all … of her books. I've recently finished *The Funicular Trampoline*. I just love her style. Easy but deep … [I've never heard *that* before; must remember it for mum] … what's her latest?'

'*Tales from an Elephant's Rucksack*. But it's not finished yet. I think it'll be out later next year.'

'I'll look out for it.'

'Right. You might even meet mum if you're here a bit later on.'

Later in the day, Hannah was sitting in her chair when her mum and Frankie came in: 'Hello Darling!'

'Hey mum, Frank … good to see you both.'

'I've brought you a present,' said Frankie, producing a pair of crutch-covers she'd designed, and made of fake 'ocelot' fur. 'Hope you like the material.'

'Brilliant,' said Hannah as Frankie fitted the covers to her crutches with Velcro. 'Really upmarket stuff. I'll call them my "ocelots".'

'Anyway, how are you feeling today?' asked her mum.

'A lot better … went for a bit of a walk around yesterday … met a nice boy too!'

Frankie smiled: 'Ah yes … the one you were telling me about

… Ben? … is that his name?'

'Yes – Ben Riley. Mum … he's had an ileostomy.'

'Crikey! And how's he doing?'

'He's doing well. He should be discharged any time now.'

'Did he tell you what an ileostomy is?'

Hannah explained as best she could.

'So where did you meet him?'

'On a bench outside in the grounds. I was resting after a bit of a walk, and he just came and sat with me and we got chatting.'

'Oh … that's nice.'

'It's weird. It made me realise … he'd never seen me with two legs … and he didn't seem too bothered about me having only one either …'

'Yes … People aren't fazed by that sort of thing in hospital. But I guess it may change the way you meet new people now … and the way new people get to know you … and maybe even *why*.'

'Anyway … I went to see Ben today … he's on this level in a ward across the corridor – Sycamore.'

'Oh, that was nice of you.'

'Yeah … well, I liked him. I met his Ma too. She's nice as well. In fact she mentioned you, mum …'

'Really?'

'Yes … she's read … umm … most of your books … so she says … likes your style … *easy but deep*, that's how she put it.'

'Oh … nice. Never thought of it quite like that.'

As if on a cue, at that moment Ben appeared and invited them all to join him and his mum in the day-room for afternoon tea, where Mrs Riley was anxious to meet Jill, and they talked books well into the evening.

∞

A couple of days later Miss Pembrey inspected Hannah's stump before saying that she could go home as soon as her stitches had been removed and her mum had been through the discharge checklist with Staff Nurse Moira. The removal of the forty-nine stitches gave Hannah a very odd tweaking feeling in her stump, but she felt a step nearer to her new self. She put on her blue denim trousers and green top, with a stripy green sock and snug-fitting trainer in anticipation of her return home.

As Staff Nurse Moira went through dressings, shrinkers and ointments with Jill, Frankie helped Hannah gather everything she'd accumulated during her stay. Hannah allowed Frankie to pull up her left trouser-leg and arrange it neatly into her waistband at the back. As she stood, she realised how very one-legged the adjusted trouser-leg made her feel.

Patsy the physio appeared, and Hannah explained about the stairlift at home, to persuade her to produce another pair of crutches for use upstairs. Patsy agreed, and then went on to discuss Hannah's programme of rehab visits, and the forthcoming work in the prosthetic department. Then Hannah remembered Ben and excused herself so that she could go to say good-bye to him.

Ben was quite surprised and a little disappointed that Hannah was going home before he was. Unfortunately, that was the moment that Tracy Wright, who lived next door to Ben and thought of him as her property, appeared at the door of the ward and saw her boyfriend being embraced by a one-legged girl with copious red hair – it could only be the girl whose accident she'd read about in the paper. Boiling with rage, she retreated at high speed, vowing to sort Hannah out, not understanding the hospital camaraderie that had prompted their apparent intimacy.

Hannah knew nothing of this, of course, and returned to Hyacinth to find that Patsy had produced the spare pair of crutches she had asked for, and that her mum and Frankie were packed up and ready to leave. She spurned the offer of being pushed in the wheelchair in favour of her crutches and stepped out confidently.

Jill pushed the wheelchair loaded with Hannah's belongings, and Hannah experienced a slight fluttering of her heart; she had walked down this corridor and back many times for crutch practice, but now she was free; she was about to face the *real* world – not the hospital world – missing a leg, and she wondered what it was really going to be like. Frankie and her mum walked behind talking quietly ... that's our lovely Hannah ... now she's only got one leg ... how will she adjust to this new way of life? ... how will it affect her? ... how will it affect us? ... what's going to happen over the next few days? ... weeks? ... months?

They entered the lift and descended to the reception area. Frankie stayed with Hannah while their mum went to fetch the car, noting that her O-L sister appeared to have become an object of interest to many of the people milling about.

When the car arrived, Hannah crutched out and gingerly lowered herself into the front seat, helping her Precious in and pivoting carefully. Meanwhile, Frankie had unloaded the wheelchair, and expertly folded it into the boot.

Riding in a car – another first. Hannah was suddenly so pleased to be back in the real world: 'Wowee! This is the beginning of my new O-L life. Just got to get on with it now. Hope you're cool with it. Oh! One thing I notice ...'

'Yes?'

'The traffic seems to be whizzing really fast.'

'Yes ...'

Hannah closed her eyes; when she opened them again, they were turning into the drive of Victoria House.

She did her best to emerge elegantly from the car; Jill opened the boot and started to unload her things: 'Han, I'll help you in a moment ... oh!'

Jill was surprised and disconcerted when Hannah hopped round to help her. She extracted the ocelots: 'Well ... here are my ocelots, so these others must be the ones for upstairs ... oh!'

Olivia appeared from the house and they exchanged welcoming hugs: 'Come round here ...' It felt as though they hadn't seen each other for ever.

Suddenly there was a shout: 'Surprise!'

'DAD!'

Martin and Hannah hugged.

⁊〰

On the back terrace, Olivia had laid out cold drinks and nibbles. Jill sat down under the parasol: 'I thought we'd sit here for a few minutes ... if that's OK. Sort out the domestic things. Put your crutches in the pot there, Hannah. Dad rescued a few from one of his clients who was moving. Olivia decorated them, so now they're just the job for your crutches – crutchpots.'

Hannah obediently stood her crutches in the pot and hopped over to the swing seat with its striped awning; she beckoned to Frankie to sit by her.

While Olivia was busy with the drinks, Hannah looked at her mum: 'Domestic things?'

'Umm ... yes. You'll have to work out new ways of doing some things, won't you?'

'Probably,' said Hannah. 'How I do things, fetch things, where we put the crutchpots, that sort of thing you mean?'

'Yes. We've had the wenteltrap serviced ...'

'Trusty old stairlift ...'

Glasses were filled with apple juice or ginger beer. At last, Martin appeared and, ever the master of ceremonies, even in adversity, raised a glass aloft: 'I'd like to say how pleased I am – we all are – that Hannah's home again.'

'Hear, hear ...'

Martin gave Hannah a quick welcoming hug and ceremoniously handed her a little zipped purse, in which she found a shiny new key-ring with a tag engraved with her name and bearing not only her house keys, but another rather larger key.

'WOW!! Thanks *soooo* much, dad. What's this funny one?'

'Ahh! ... Passport to happiness ... what they call a Radar key – to open disabled loos throughout the land.'

'Thanks, dad. You think of everything. Have you come home for long?'

'Only for a few days; I'm in the middle of a research contract ...'

'And you have to get back,' put in Jill, thinking that at some point she'd have to explain to the girls what she'd found out about their father.

⁊⊃

After lunch, Hannah wriggled on to the stairlift – the first time ever with one leg, and up she went. Jill had already placed her upstairs crutches in another crutchpot on the landing. Once they were firmly in her hands, she made her way to her room: 'Looks exactly the same ... and why not? God, I'm so glad to be back home,' she thought. She dropped her crutches and hopped over to her bed and lay down, trying to take in every detail.

The room had a glow to it. Having been away for what felt like an eternity, Hannah felt that the colours had got brighter and the edges sharper – perhaps in contrast to the whiteness of her hospital room. Her senses felt more alive than ever before. She noted the freshly laundered sheets. Her eye fell on her wall calendar that still showed 8 August. And now it was 23 August. What a lot had happened in a fortnight!

Hannah took off her trousers and shrinker, and got out the mirror from her bedside drawer to inspect her stump. It was the first time she'd had a chance to inspect all round it in privacy, and her head swam as she realised again that what she saw was now her shape *for ever*. She had no left leg. The end of her stump looked somewhat crinkly, with little puckers where the stitches had been. Amazing how rapidly such a gross wound healed. Granted, the stump was a strange shape, but then everyone at Jimmy's had told her that 'it' was doing well, and that 'it' would take a little time to 'settle down'.

Tears appeared in the corners of her eyes as Frankie looked in to see what was happening; she was taken aback to see Hannah's bare stump at home for the first time. Her heart gave a leap as she sat by Hannah on the bed, put her arms around her and gave her a big hug: 'It's OK. It's all gonna be OK. There's nothing to worry about, we're all here for you, every step … [ouch] … of the way'

'I … kn … ow … it's just …'

'You've done bl*ooo*dy well so far, Madam. Don't know how you've got this far without breaking down.'

'I've been … trying … hard … really hard.'

'I know. We all know. It's OK. Let it all out, it's better than bottling it all up.'

'Thanks … Frank … thanks.'

'Anything for you Han; I'll do *any*thing.'

'Thanks again.'

Frankie cuddled her sister till Hannah dropped off to sleep and then stayed beside her on the bed. She lay still but wide awake, thinking about all the obstacles Hannah would have to overcome in the coming weeks. She heard their mum calling but was loath to wake her: 'I think mum's made tea,' she said. 'Shall we go down?'

'Yeah …' replied a groggy Hannah. She sat up, put her clothes on again, and pulled down her top: 'Frank …?'

'Yip?'

'Will you help me take a shower later on?'

'Of course. Up we get … Let me tuck your leg in again …'

Hannah made her way to the stairlift, whirred downstairs, crutched to the kitchen, dropped her crutches into the convenient crutchpot, hopped over to her mum, and gave her a big hug and a kiss. This was the first time that her mum had seen her hopping freely over any distance, and it brought home to her again the reality that Hannah's loss was permanent; she turned away to hide the tears in her eyes, but she knew she had to be strong.

Hannah sat at the big scrubbed table with a mug of tea, watching her mum cooking: 'Wow, that smells scrumpsh!'

'Thank you Han. The Brooks Special – curried chicken with egg fried rice, Bombay potatoes and naan bread … fancy any poppadoms?'

'That's more than plenty, mum … you could cook for an army … but pops always welcome.'

'OK then, better call the troops!'

Retrieving her trusty ocelots, Hannah went off to find Olivia, who had taken her laptop into the cool of the music room, and dug her dad out of his study.

'So good to have Han home again,' said her mum to Frankie later.

'Isn't it great?' said Frankie. '*Almost* as if nothing had happened.'

# 9

## Tracy Wright

**A**wakening slowly on her first morning home, Hannah took some time to realise where she was before savouring the joy of finding herself in her own bed again, hating the fact that she had to use the commode. No sooner had she started to think about how she was going to spend the day, than there was a knock on the door and Frankie entered with a welcome mug of tea.

Frankie wanted to make everything as easy as possible for her sister. It soon dawned on Hannah that nothing was going to be exactly as it had been before her accident, and that whatever she wanted to do, she would have to work out first how she was going to do it. The thought terrified her.

Although she could use her wheelchair or her crutches, or hop or crawl, she would have to think ahead about whatever she needed for her next manoeuvre. Frankie was intrigued by the problems raised, and together they started to consider what items Hannah might usefully carry with her. The list became longer and longer, and wilder and wilder, until they dissolved into gales of laughter.

∽

First, Hannah had to think about what she was going to wear that day, and this led them to consider how best to arrange her clothes, her make-up and her jewellery. Then, in the bathroom, every action needed serious consideration.

When at last they descended to the kitchen for breakfast, they chatted on about how Hannah could live an ordinary everyday life as an O-L-er, returning to their favourite subject of Hannah's wardrobe. They wondered about the possibility of visiting an amputee shoe exchange, but Frankie was concerned that Hannah should not do too much too soon.

The following afternoon, Hannah set out on her first walk outdoors on her own – just up Victoria Road, round Albert Avenue and home, with the hidden agenda that she might see Ben, who lived somewhere in Albert Avenue. She had told Frankie of her plan, but refused any assistance her sister offered.

When she reached the corner of Victoria Road, she came across her friend Jo pushing her bicycle. Jo Tomlinson had been in her tutor group at College: 'Hi ... Hannah ... Look at you! I heard you'd had an accident. What happened? Oh my God! You really *have* lost a leg just like they said, haven't you! Ouch! That's terrible. How's it going?' She babbled on, afraid to say the wrong thing.

'Going? It's gone. But it's cool. Once you realise there's no going back, and you just have to get on with your new life, it gets easier. Well, a bit ...'

'Umm ... Does it ... hurt at all?'

'Certainly does ... and I sometimes get funny feelings in the leg that isn't there – phantom sensations, they're called.'

'I've heard about that – weird ... so what will you do ... when you're ... better?'

'What's "better"?'

'Umm ... [embarrassed] ... I suppose "better" would be getting your leg back.'

'That's true! At the moment I'm concentrating on physio. And I was planning to take a year out anyway, so I don't suppose I'll miss much.'

'And are you getting a new leg? If you don't mind my asking.'

'That's OK. Not ready for it yet – a new leg, that is. Do you realise, I have to work out every little thing I'm going to do before I do it. I've got more than enough to think about, just settling into my new way of life, thank you. But I can get along pretty well as I am.'

'So I see. Hope you didn't mind me asking. We two-legged people … umm … guess we've got a lot to learn.'

'Cool … glad you see it that way. There aren't too many of us O-L-ers – one-leggers – about, I can tell you.'

'Really? I think you're the first person with one leg I've ever met. Course, I've seen athletes and soldiers with limbs missing on the telly. But it does take a bit of getting used to seeing you like that. Especially as I knew you when you had two legs. Umm … do you think it's different if you see someone you *don't* know with one leg?'

'Possibly. I'm ready for people to freak out when they see me like this. But nobody has yet. Even people who know … knew … me. Like you.'

'Ah! But it's just a leg, isn't it? It's still you inside, isn't it?'

'Yes it is! Thanks … it means such a lot to me when you say that,' said Hannah. 'I'm soooo glad you see it like that.' She hoped other people would react in the same way.

Jo pushed her bicycle on to the road, painfully aware of how difficult – impossible – it would be to manage a bicycle if you had only one leg. Hannah made a show of not noticing Jo's awkwardness.

Continuing along Albert Avenue, shaded by its plane trees, Hannah suddenly came across Ben proudly but needlessly polishing his motorcycle on the paved area in front of his house. His back was turned; she approached as quietly as possible. 'Guess who?'

Ben swung round in surprise, and hugged Hannah joyfully;

Hannah dropped her crutches, lost her balance, and grabbed Ben's motorcycle. Instinctively, Ben grabbed hold of them both and Hannah somehow ended up perched on the saddle.

'You look just right on there,' said Ben. 'As soon as I get another crash helmet, I'll take you for a spin.'

Hannah wasn't sure that she wanted to take advantage of the offer, but kept her thoughts to herself.

Tracy Wright, the somewhat odd girl who lived next door to Ben and so assumed that she must be his girlfriend, chose that moment to look out of her window and see Ben and the one-legged girl with red hair once again engaged in conversation. She became the victim of instant fury, remembering her vow in the hospital to sort that girl out for daring to hug Ben.

Knowing she was alone in the house, Tracy made her way to the drinks cupboard and took a couple of supportive swigs of drambuie, being careful to leave everything as she had found it.

She had little idea of what she was going to do, but now felt hugely confident about anything. As the drambuie took its warming effect, she slipped out of the back door and made her way along the back path known as Dennett's Drift, a leafy lane that ran parallel to Albert Avenue as far as the bottle banks that stood down the road discreetly behind a screening hedge.

She was relying on the one-legged girl coming past the recycling bay; meanwhile she inspected the bottles that were spilling out of the bins and standing around in plastic bags to see if she could find anything potable.

Becoming bolder and less coherent as the alcohol raced

around her system, Tracy peeped round the screening hedge from time to time, until at last she was rewarded with the sight of her victim-to-be crutching along the road towards her. She still had no plan, but was sure something would occur to her when the time came. As she judged that the girl was getting closer, she strolled nonchalantly and unsteadily out on to the Albert Avenue pavement and leant against the screening hedge, ready to confront her.

'I suppose you think that you can steal anyone you want for yourself, just because you've got one leg,' Tracy growled.

'I'm sorry?' Hannah failed to make sense of Tracy's verbal attack; her reply was delivered somewhat too softly.

Tracy tried again: 'Just because you've got one leg, you needn't think you can steal anyone you want for yourself, Princess Pity.'

Hannah had no idea what Tracy meant, and from the slurring of her voice realised that asking her to explain would be pointless.

She tried to carry on past Tracy, hoping Tracy would leave her be, but Tracy stepped into her path and held her arms wide apart to form a barrier. Forced to stop in her tracks, rather than step into the road, Hannah automatically held up her right crutch in front of her to fend Tracy off, whereupon Tracy grabbed hold of it and wrenched it from Hannah's grasp. Hannah threw away her other crutch and used both arms to steady herself against the rather too scratchy screening hedge to make her inevitable collapse to the ground less painful. She ended up sitting on the pavement leaning against the hedge, while Tracy retrieved her other crutch and tossed them both into a handy skip that stood by the bottle bank.

Tracy towered over Hannah and hissed: 'That'll teach you.' She aimed a kick or two at her, which fortunately missed her stump – although they did give her right knee a nasty jolt.

'Teach me what?' asked Hannah, thinking she might as well try and find out what she was supposed to have done. But by then Tracy was making her way unsteadily home.

As Tracy reached her house, Ben was still needlessly polishing his motorbike.

She turned towards him and with a malicious grin snarled: 'That's well and truly put that one-legged cow out of action,' stumbling indoors before Ben could fathom what she meant.

Not suspecting that Tracy had just attacked Hannah, let alone that she had seen them together, Ben couldn't fail to pick up on the phrase 'one-legged cow'. Secretly glad of an excuse for a bike-ride, he set off down Albert Avenue to seek out clues as to what Tracy was talking about.

As she rested against the hedge getting her breath back, Hannah's stump filled with waves of searing pains – real and phantom – and her head filled with jumbled thoughts. What was all that about? Who was that girl? Why was she so antagonistic towards her? What would happen if she tried to stand up, hop to the skip [she gave a little laugh at the phrase], dive in and retrieve her crutches? What else was in the skip, and how full was it? If she did manage to get into it, would she be able to get out again? Would her crutches have suffered any damage? The pain in her right knee as a result of the kicking was now making itself felt – and there was also substantial throbbing in her stump. If she could stand up again, and retrieve her crutches, would she be able to walk properly anyway?

Then she heard the sound of a motorbike approaching. Ben pulled up with a screech, hardly believing his eyes, and in an instant parked his bike, saw that Hannah was in distress and in an instant was kneeling down comforting her and trying to piece together her story.

He helped her up to sit more comfortably on a low wall, and was outraged when he heard what had happened. Hannah persuaded him to cool down and concentrate on sorting her out. She pointed out the skip in which her crutches turned out to lie in a muddy puddle. Ben went to fish them out, found a piece of old towel to wipe them clean as best he could, and returned them to Hannah triumphantly. She felt an instant wave of relief.

The attack had really shaken her up, and she realised how impotent and isolated she felt without her crutches. She tried to explain this to Ben, but he didn't appear to understand the full significance of what she was trying to say.

Suddenly Ben kissed her; he was appalled as he registered the muddy footprints on her right trouser-leg: 'Looks as if you've had a bit of a kicking,' he said. 'How are you feeling now?'

'Still achey,' replied Hannah. 'But a lot better than I did before you showed up. Do you know who that awful girl was? Have you any idea what that was all about?'

'I think it was Tracy Wright' said Ben. 'She lives next door to me, but I have no idea why she attacked you. All I know is, she staggered home a few minutes ago.'

'I thought she was drunk,' said Hannah. 'But if she lives next door …'

'I'll try and find out,' said Ben. 'But anyway, let me take you home and sort you out.'

Ben helped Hannah on to his pillion seat – not too difficult with a missing leg. He hoped that she wouldn't slide off equally easily, but Hannah had wedged her crutches at an angle and carefully put Ben's crash helmet on, whereupon she felt isolated from the world.

Mrs Riley was surprised to see Hannah crutching in through the back door, as Ben explained that she'd had a bit of an accident and had come in to get her breath back.

'Tea or coffee or something else?' she enquired.

'Umm … coffee, please,' said Hannah. 'May I sit down?'

'Of course, of course … whatever's happened to your trousers?'

Hannah felt rather cagy about explaining in detail what had happened, but Mrs Riley came at her with a stiff brush and was able to remove much of the drying mud.

'That's better,' she said.

'At least she missed my stump,' shuddered Hannah, 'but my knee's a bit stiff.'

Ben was still thinking about their respective surgeries, wondering what Hannah's wound looked like compared with his. Then he returned to the present: 'So, how far from here to where you live?'

Hannah explained where Victoria House was, and suddenly realised she'd walked quite a way.

There was a knocking at the back door; Mrs Riley opened it to see a crestfallen Tracy standing there: 'Come in, come in. What would you like? Tea or coffee or something else?' she enquired.

Tracy made a mumbling noise and slumped into a chair, refusing to look at the red-haired girl sitting opposite. She hung her head and slouched in silence.

Knowing nothing of what had happened, Mrs Riley went over to comfort her. 'It can't be that bad,' she said.

'Oh yes it can!' said Tracy. 'A lot worse. I've been a … I don't know what I've been.'

'Tracy, this is Hannah,' said Ben. 'We met in hospital. Is it true that you attacked her down the road just now? Whatever did you think you were doing?'

'I saw her hugging you in hospital,' said Tracey. 'I'd come to see you but I just couldn't take it.'

'Well, it was very nice of you to think of visiting me, even if you didn't get that far – I'd only just met Hannah, and she was about to be discharged from hospital and you must have seen her coming to say good-bye to me.'

'And then today I was just going for a walk, and found Ben with his motorbike,' said Hannah. 'I couldn't ignore him … could I?'

'I think I've made an idiot of myself,' admitted Tracy. 'I'm not really as awful as …' Amid billows of sobs she tried to explain herself, failing miserably, and managing only to convey the very basics of what had crossed her mind.

Mrs Riley was still in comforting mode, and ushered Tracy into the lounge, and away from Ben and Hannah.

There was an awkward silence in the kitchen, until Ben spoke up: 'Will you take a chance with no helmet and let me run you home?' he asked. 'Well, you can wear the helmet, and I'll take the chance,' he chuckled.

'That would be good,' said Hannah. 'I don't want to worry anyone from home by asking them to come and help me. But I won't ask you in, if you don't mind. There'll be enough to contend with anyway, if they find out what happened, and I don't want to have to deal with that.'

'Drop me off out here, please,' said Hannah. But her attempt at concealing that something had happened was to no avail, as there was her mum weeding a flower-bed; she looked up when she heard the motorbike: 'Hello, Ben,' she called, 'glad to see you're out of hospital,' and then she saw her daughter on the pillion behind Ben.

'I've brought Hannah home,' announced Ben. 'Rescued her, and brought her home.'

'What on earth's happened?' asked Jill. 'You'd better come in and tell us all about it.'

Hannah scowled.

୫

When Hannah removed her trousers she was shocked to see the marks made by Tracy's foot. She rubbed some soothing cream into the bruise on her knee, and changed into her frilly blue denim skirt.

Downstairs, Jill, Hannah and Ben were seated around the table, when Frankie came in. 'Ben!' she exclaimed, 'How nice to see you. Why are you here?'

'Well …' said Ben, not sure what he might say that wouldn't hurt Hannah.

But Hannah took over: 'I met a strange girl who must have mistaken me for someone else because she attacked me. But then she made off and Ben came along and brought me home and no harm done.'

'How do you mean, she attacked you?' asked Frankie, incensed.

'Nothing terrible,' said Hannah, 'and Ben soon came along and sorted it all out.'

'Do you think we should go to the police?' asked Jill.

'Oh, no, no, no, no, no,' said Hannah.

'Hmm …' said Ben, 'She won't do it again, I guess. Best forget about it.' He wanted to show Hannah he understood and swiftly changed the subject to Jill's gardening, so thoughts of Tracy rapidly faded into the background.

# 10

## Lorna Macey

The 'For Sale' card on the noticeboard advertised 'a pair of antique rosewood crutches'. They sounded so exotic that Frankie immediately thought she should get them as an unexpected present for Hannah. She got out her mobile and rang the number there and then, before setting off on her bicycle, and soon arriving at a large house in Nightingale Avenue, similar to Victoria House but with a smaller garden and hardly any outbuildings.

Lorna Macey, tall and formally dressed, ushered Frankie into a sitting-room full of heavy Victorian furniture. Frankie had the feeling that time stood still in this house; she felt as though she were in a different world – which she found rather pleasant.

She was surprised that Miss Macey – Lorna – wasn't old as well, like the furniture.

After some small-talk Lorna got to the point: 'Well, I expect you'd like to see the antique rosewood crutches that brought you here.'

'Yes, please,' said Frankie, 'I certainly would.'

'And may I ask what your interest is?'

'Yes … my sister Hannah recently lost a leg in a road accident and I thought a pair of exotic crutches – well, they sound exotic – might … amuse her. Assuming they're the right size, of course.'

'Oh my dear!' exclaimed Lorna, 'What happened to her?'

So Frankie explained about Hannah's accident, and Lorna left the room for a moment; then returned with a pair of axillary crutches and held them out to Frankie, who leapt to her feet letting out an enormous: 'Wow! I didn't realise they'd be like this.'

'Oh,' said Lorna, 'what *were* you expecting, then?'

'Umm ... some sort of ordinary crutches like you get these days, only made of ... er ... rosewood. These ones are more Long John Silvery sort of things.'

Lorna looked a little put out: 'You have to realise that these are antique,' she said. 'A pair of crutches like they used to be. These were made well before the Second World War. Possibly before the First. They may be a century old or more.'

Frankie examined the crutches and saw that they seemed to be perfectly in keeping with the room's Victorian décor and theme – with their rosewood staves and padded tops of polished maroon leather fastened with shiny brass upholstery studs, and their lower ends furnished with somewhat incongruous brand-new grey non-slip tips. Yet in spite of their appearing so solid, Frankie was amazed at how light they were when she picked them up. She was slightly worried because they appeared to have no means of adjustment; she put them under her arms to try them for size: 'I *think* they'll be OK,' she said, taking a few steps on them, 'but I expect we can find a way of adjusting them if needed. The grain and colour of the wood are fantastic. Perhaps they're *meant*.'

'I'm a firm believer in things being *meant*,' said Lorna, somewhat mollified. 'Now, I'll show you something else.'

She produced an old photograph in a beautiful polished rosewood frame that matched the crutches. Frankie drew in a sharp breath, as she saw a good-looking young woman with one leg, wearing what she thought must be her best dress and supported on what she was certain must be the very crutches she was now holding.

'Those crutches you have there, the ones in the picture, belonged to my granny, Delia Winchester,' explained Lorna. 'I could get you a copy of this photo to go with the crutches. Perhaps Harriet would appreciate that?'

'Hannah,' Frankie corrected. 'Thanks very much, I'm sure she would.' Thoughts crowded into her head: 'Is your granny still alive?' she asked wonderingly.

'No, she's died, but she left me this house and everything in it, including her collection of things associated with having one leg. But I've got a house already, and I'm downsizing here so that I can move back,' said Lorna.

Frankie had a fleeting image of Hannah as an old lady. She thought for a moment before questioning Lorna – 'Can you tell me a bit more about your granny?' she asked. 'I'm sure Hannah would like to know …' Privately, she wanted to know as well.

'Of course,' said Lorna, 'Granny seldom talked about her early life, but I know she was born in Coventry, and I know she lost her right leg in the air raid when the Cathedral was hit during the Second World War. That raid also took the rest of her family, except her elder brother who was away on war work and her father who was away in the RAF. After granny came out of hospital, she went to live with her Auntie Lavender – somewhere in Leicestershire, I think. And later she became the joint owner of a garden centre with her husband, which my uncle now runs. And that's about all I know. She hardly talked about it at all.'

'After the war her elder brother – my great-uncle – emigrated to New Zealand and disappeared, and great-grandfather married again and eventually granny and her daughter – my mother – came to live here. I grew up here and when my mother, and later my father, died, I moved back home to be with granny. And now she's gone.'

Frankie thought about how lonely it must be to have no family.

'Of course,' went on Lorna, 'they are quite old-fashioned – the crutches, I mean – but granny loved them, and kept them polished for special occasions – in fact, she once met the Queen on them. But actually, *she* was given them by a Lady Morris who had one leg – don't ask me who she was, or why she had one leg, or even how she knew granny and why she gave her a pair of crutches …

but that's where they came from, and they were always known as "Lady M's crutches", or "the Lady Ms." I don't really know much about them, now that I think about it.'

Frankie laughed: 'I guess with all that history – and the photos – Hannah'll *really* feel like a member of the one-legged sisterhood. She likes that sort of thing.'

'Hannah sounds quite special,' said Lorna. 'I'd like to meet her because I've got various other things that might be of interest to her.'

'That sounds great,' said Frankie. 'But … how much do you want for the crutches?'

'Oh … I'd be so pleased for Hannah just to *have* them … I'd just like them to go to a good home.'

'Thank you very much,' said Frankie. 'If you're sure that's OK.'

'That's settled, then. Tell you what, give me a ring so we can fix a time for Hannah to come round, and we can go through the other things of granny's that might be useful – or interesting – to her. And I'll get her a copy of the photo.'

'Thanks. I'm sure she'd like that.'

℘

Back at Victoria House, Frankie stood with the rosewood crutches under her arms and called Hannah.

'I've bought – brought – you a present, Han.'

'That's kind …? Wow!' Hannah's eyes lit up; she leant her ocelots against the sofa, hopped over to her sister, positioned the rosewood crutches under her own arms, and stepped tentatively round the room: 'Axillary crutches,' she said, 'I've never tried this sort of crutches before, and these are … magnificent … incredibly … comfortable. And just the right height, luckily, since they appear to have no adjustment. Umm … they're actually what Meg Brown was talking about that time she came to see me in ozzy.'

113

'Oh? What was that, then?'

'She said that Dolores would kill her – Meg – for telling me about axillary crutches, but they could be … amazingly useful about the house – cleaning, cooking, housework, all that sort of domestic stuff. She said that you can squeeze them between your upper arms and the sides of your body, and walk without holding them with your hands. And you can walk on a single crutch of this sort – I'll have to try that. You can even carry other stuff. Could get interesting.'

Hannah swung over to Frankie, and gave her an enormous hug; then went to see their mum and Olivia in the kitchen. Both admired the Lady Ms, and were intrigued to hear about Lorna Macey and her granny.

'And how did her granny lose her leg?' asked Olivia.

'We didn't talk much about that,' said Frankie; 'but it seems that she was injured during the air raid when Coventry Cathedral was destroyed.'

❦

Hannah soon got the measure of the Lady Ms, but found them very intractable. The elbow crutches she normally used allowed her body and arms much more flexibility – particularly on stairs – and she failed to understand why the axillary crutch design had been so popular and so widely used – and sometimes was still.

She persevered with the Lady Ms because they looked so beautiful. Meg had said you could walk on a single axillary crutch, so she decided to experiment with that. Choosing one of the Lady Ms, she thought about what she needed to do.

Bracing herself, she stood up and snuggled the crutch into position under her left arm. The saddle had a deep depression to keep the crutch in position, and she found that there was quite high friction between the covering of the saddle and her clothing

– presumably for the same reason. Holding her breath, she stepped the crutch forward, and then concentrated on moving her foot to catch up. Rather clumsily, she hopped her foot forward. Suddenly, she remembered what Meg had said: 'The secret lies in placing the end of the crutch where your foot would be if you still had it. Then pivot slightly on the crutch as you step your actual leg forward. That's how you can walk smoothly … it's not at all the same as walking on two crutches … with just one, you've got to try and use it as your missing leg and not as a crutch … and not to hop, but to … *step.*'

As she practised with the single crutch, she decided to call it Hoppy when used in that way.

In came Frankie: 'Gosh, that looks pretty amazing,' she said.

'Oh, Frank, look …'

Hannah took a few steps; then stood to talk to Frankie: 'It *is* tiring, but I know I'll get better and better at it, and it'll certainly be useful …'

℘

Hannah thought that the sooner they went back to see Lorna the better – apart from anything else, she wanted to find out what other goodies Lorna's granny had to offer. Olivia was intrigued to hear about Frankie's visit, and offered to drive them over to see Lorna.

As they arrived the next Saturday, Lorna opened the front door to see Hannah approaching on the Lady Ms. Delighted at the sight, she gave the girls tea and biscuits, and then suggested they should go upstairs where she kept all her granny's stuff.

'Can you manage the stairs OK?' asked Lorna. 'Granny used to scare me stiff going up and down stairs on crutches, but perhaps …'

'I'll go on one and the handrail,' said Hannah comfortably. She transferred both axillaries to her left hand and up she went.

'In here,' said Lorna, throwing open a door further down the corridor. There, on what they guessed must have been granny's bed, were several pairs of modern elbow crutches decorated in various ways, another six pairs of axillary crutches – nothing as as pretty – or as comfortable-looking – as the Lady Ms – and some single axillary crutches.

Lorna drew their attention to the somewhat crude pair that granny had first been given in hospital, without any instruction on how to use them, or counselling on having lost a leg: 'as I'm sure you'd get nowadays,' said Lorna. 'Granny said she felt thoroughly bewildered when she woke up in hospital and only gradually came to understand what had happened to her, and then had to work out how to do everything on one leg.'

Hannah knew how granny must have felt, and wondered whether, when she herself had been an O-L-er all her life, she would have acquired as many pairs of crutches. 'Why did she have so many pairs?' she ventured.

'Good question,' said Lorna. 'All I know is that she claimed she got as much pleasure from having a new pair of crutches to match a new outfit as someone else might get from a new pair of shoes. But look at these – child's elbow crutches with red, yellow, blue and green plastic fittings, *and* red reflectors in the handgrips: great idea. No good to granny of course, but she just loved the thought that had gone into their design.

'Granny often used a single crutch to get about, like round the house or in the garden. But, of course, a single modern forearm crutch by itself wouldn't be any good unless you were using it to steady yourself; it has to be an axillary sort to fit under the arm. That's why those odd ones are all axillaries.'

Hannah picked up one and tried it, pottering round the room: 'This is all pretty new to me,' she said. 'I have tried one like this, but I need loads more practice before I can actually go anywhere.

Good job I'm the same height as your granny.' She took an awkward step or two: 'Hmm ...'

'I see you've lost your left leg, opposite to granny,' said Lorna. 'And granny kept all the right shoes she didn't use ... I don't suppose ...' She produced a box of unworn right shoes.

'Well,' said Hannah, sitting on the bed and trying on a shoe at random, 'these ... fit ... OK. They're old-fashioned – but all brand new, never been used.'

'You might as well take them all,' said Lorna, producing another two boxes of unworn right shoes.'

'Thanks,' said Hannah. When she wore them, she could explain proudly that they were vintage.

She noticed two old-fashioned folded wheelchairs, some padded perching stools, and some artificial legs. The height of the stools was just right: 'This one is really comfortable,' she said, sitting on it: 'I suppose your granny used it in the kitchen.'

'Kitchen, bathroom, all over the place,' said Lorna. 'In the kitchen she often pulled out a drawer to rest what she called her "short leg" on. I expect you find you have to improvise like that yourself ... And I don't know if you're interested, but here,' went on Lorna, 'are some prostheses – artificial legs – granny acquired over the years. She tended to wear them when she went out – sometimes when she was very tired I'd push her in a wheelchair with a fake leg on and nobody would give her a second glance.'

'I see ...,' mused Hannah. That could stop some of the staring.

'And here,' continued Lorna, 'are some peg legs – I do believe this ... [she held up a curious-looking artefact] ... is the very first artificial leg she ever had, made for her by the village basketmaker during the war, fairly soon after she'd lost her leg, when she went to live with her Auntie Lavender. Auntie Lavender knitted her thick socks of green wool for the stump of her leg so that she could snuggle it into the woven cane socket at the end of the fake leg ... here. [Lorna passed it to Hannah.] And this is a leg granny used about the house and garden a lot when she was younger, but … I suppose these wouldn't be much good to you?'

'Interesting,' said Hannah. 'It's possible … I think really we should keep the collection together.' She picked up the leg made by the village basketmaker all those years ago and before her very eyes, it turned into a work of folk art that had enabled a young girl injured in the war to walk again. In that moment, she felt curiously close to Lorna's granny, and gave a little shudder. She promised herself that she'd see if she could put it to use again and keep the history alive.

'Please keep the collection together,' said Lorna. 'I know that's what granny would have liked. And then,' went on Lorna, bringing her back to earth, 'here are some copies of photos for you. These are of granny – here she is in her best frock with the crutches you're using now, and here's one of Lady M herself, who gave them to granny. But I don't really know who Lady M was, and I expect it's far too late to find out, as she was older than granny.'

The picture showed a one-legged woman in her gardening clothes, with the right leg of her trousers pinned up over the stump of her leg with a decorative kilt pin, and wearing an enormous hat, looking surprisingly petite to be in charge of an even more enormous ride-on lawnmower.

'What I don't have,' went on Lorna. 'Is a picture of Lady M on the Lady Ms … at least, I haven't found one yet …'

'It would be nice,' said Hannah. 'Sort of complete the circle.'

'Now,' said Lorna, 'here are some books with amputees in them. The very earliest was published in 1851 – *Moby Dick*, by Herman Melville.'

'I've heard of that, and seen the film,' said Hannah. I'd forgotten it came from a book. And then there's Stevenson's *Treasure Island*, of course.'

'Yes. And here's the anonymous *The Girl with the Rosewood*

*Crutches* which dates from 1912: I don't know anything much about that.'

'I'll read it and let you know, then,' said Hannah, 'if you mean me to take this little library over.'

'Surely – I hope you will. This book is *Out on a Limb* by Louise Baker. She lost her leg when she took a forbidden bike-ride when she was eight, and spent the rest of a light-hearted life on crutches. The book dates from 1946, and it seems it was promoted by the US Government as a boost to servicemen who had lost a leg in the War.'

Lorna selected an album of photos and handed it to the girls. 'Now these here are very interesting – I think. Granny belonged to an organisation called *AAA – Amputee Artistes' Association*. The album was open at a picture showing a road-accident victim whose leg appeared to have been torn off. The girls felt sick; Hannah nearly passed out – at first she thought it was her, but didn't see how it could be when she looked closer; the girl was a blonde, not a redhead, and had lost her right leg: 'Omigod!'

'So sorry, I should have warned you,' said Lorna mischievously. 'Granny used to get some film and TV work from *AAA* …'

'I see,' said Hannah, her mind racing ahead. 'Am I right in thinking that *AAA* supplies amputees for different scenarios? I'll have to look them up.'

'Granny loved "putting something back into the community",' said Lorna. 'She was a regular "victim" for paramedic training and all that sort of thing. Occasionally an extra in films. Thoroughly enjoyed it. Met some interesting people, too.'

The girls looked through the photos, which seemed a little less gruesome now that they knew what they represented, before handing the album back to Lorna.

Taking their leave, Hannah made sure that she thanked Lorna enthusiastically.

~

With all Lorna's granny's one-legged things safely in the car, Hannah reflected on the visit: 'You know, being an O-L-er seems even more difficult now. I feel as if I've entered a new country in the O-L world.'

As they carried Hannah's newly acquired objects into Victoria House, Olivia asked curiously: 'What's in that fancy wooden box? Whatever it is, it can't be very big …'

'Hadn't noticed that before,' said Hannah surprised. She opened the box to find a selection of brand-new crutch tips and some of what she thought must be the thick green woollen stump socks granny's Auntie Lavender had knitted for her during the War. There were some ornate kilt-pins, each with a label specifying 'Red trousers' or 'Purple suit' or other such item it should go with, and Hannah gave a little cry as she recognised the fancy kilt pin in the Lady M lawnmower photo. There were some photographs in a wallet, two of which she thought could only be Lady M on the Lady Ms – the missing photographs.

'I'll get copies of these for us,' she enthused. 'Lorna will be so pleased they've turned up.'

At the bottom of the box was an unassuming notebook that turned out to be a short account of Delia's life, concentrating on her wartime experiences.

Should they return it to Lorna without investigating it? That would be impossible.

The first few pages of the account contained family details: names, dates, addresses. Olivia skimmed over them while Hannah arranged herself on the sofa with a cushion on which to rest the book.

Luckily, Delia's writing was round and legible, and the girls found that they could all squeeze on to the sofa and read at the same time as Hannah.

# 11

## Delia Winchester

Now that I've retired, I think it's time to write a short memoir for the benefit of those who come after me so that they know something of my story - a bit of family history.

I was born Delia Beaumont in Coventry on 14 November 1927. My father Cyril was an engineer at Taylor and Dawson, one of the numerous engineering factories in the City, and my mother Ada (née Styles) brought up me and my siblings - my elder brother Kenneth and younger sister Sylvia. We also had a much older brother Donald, but we didn't see him very often, and always felt that he was a bit 'separate' from us, hence the lack of a mention.

The Second World War began on 3 September 1939 when I was 11 years old. Father had already volunteered for the R.A.F. Engineer Branch and he spent most of the war with a fighter wing in the very north of Scotland. We were proud of that.

We knew that Coventry would be a prime target for Nazi bombing because of all the engineering activity in the area. It was just a matter of time, and there were several small raids on the City before the Big One.

I became a teenager on 14 November
1940 - except that we didn't have
teenagers in those days, so I didn't work
that out until later. Anyway, apart from
being my 13th birthday, 14 November 1940
turned out to be the full moon night
of what we later came to know as the
Moonlight Sonata Raid - Mondscheinsonate,
the Nazi codename for the assault on
Coventry which will never be forgotten
particularly by anyone who lived through
it. That was the night that the Cathedral
was virtually destroyed, and the City of
Coventry just about flattened - hence the
Nazi word "coventrated" for a flattened
target.

We were in the kitchen having birthday
tea when the air-raid siren went off at
about ten to seven. We didn't take much
notice at first but then, as we looked
up, the bright moonlit sky gradually filled
with enemy aircraft, wave after wave of
them, dropping flares, bombs, everything,
the raid a whole lot heavier than anything
we'd experienced before. At last we were
all driven out of the house to huddle in
our Anderson shelter in the garden. There
was Mum, my brother Kenneth, sister
Sylvia, and me. The smell of damp earth
still haunts me to this day and the sound
of an air-raid siren still sends shivers up
my spine. The bombing went on and on,
and we were all sobbing and shaking inside

with fear and trying hard not to show it. The only slight comfort to be had lay in the glimpses we caught of the beams of 'our' searchlights criss-crossing the sky, and the sound of 'our' guns firing at the enemy aircraft.

Suddenly, Sylvia and I both wanted to go to the loo at the same time so we raced to the garden privy. That was the last time I saw her alive - ever. She won the race, so I went to the bathroom inside the house. An indoor bathroom was pretty uncommon in those days, but dad had made a lot of effort to install one. I looked out of the half-landing window as I went upstairs, and saw all the buildings silhouetted against the night sky, lit up by fierce flames, and that was when the Nazis decided to drop a bomb on our house, and it all went black and I don't remember anything else of that night at all.

When at last I became conscious again, I gradually worked out that I was in a hospital bed, swathed in bandages, and bruised and aching all over and hardly able to move. I wondered what had happened to the rest of the family, but not too hard at first because it was all too much to contend with, especially the pain. To this day, I'm not sure where the hospital I was taken to was, but I guess it must have been a safe distance from Coventry city centre.

I remember that someone came and fed me because both my hands were heavily bandaged, and there was a girl called Enid in the bed next to mine who had lost an arm in the same raid. She was also relieved that it was her left arm because she was right handed. She looked on that as a small victory for her!

Enid was really inspiring, because she was just happy to be alive, and to be able to help in the ward, rather than bemoaning the fact that she'd been injured.

Nobody told me what had happened to me or to my family, and it took me some time to work out that my right leg stopped about halfway down my thigh, and then it didn't seem to matter because I could hardly move without pain anyway. As time went on, my poor battered body started to recover and on fine days they helped me into a Bath Chair (imagine it!) and wrapped me up and pushed me out on to a balcony to enjoy the fresh air, even though it was pretty wintery.

When the bandages were at last taken off my hands, they brought me a pair of rather heavy wooden crutches (which I still keep for old times' sake, along with a lot of other artefacts) and helped me to get up on to them and start to get about. I found the crutches very difficult to handle until someone adjusted them for me, and even then they weren't great.

Then my friend Enid pointed out that the crutches were still too long, which meant that to use them to help me walk I had to spread the ends too far apart which could be dangerous because they were liable to slip out sideways. Also, I was resting my armpits on them, which someone told me could lead to something called 'crutch paralysis', which didn't sound very nice. So Enid helped me to adjust the crutches again so that they were shorter and at last I was able to use them properly.

At that time, the little bit of my right leg that remained was nearly always hurting, and I cried myself to sleep for several weeks until one night I noticed that the pain was beginning to get better. After that, I found that I had what were called phantom sensations in the parts of my leg that were missing, especially my foot and toes - that is, it felt as though those parts were still there.

I still have that original chunky pair of crutches in my collection, and though they're no longer any use to me they have a special sort of feel, and I have only to put them under my arms and grasp them tight and close my eyes to be taken back to those early days when I was getting used to having one leg. So I don't do that any more; the memories are too painful.

I was very surprised when my Auntie

Lavender Styles (my mum's sister) came
to visit me because we hadn't seen her
that often. She suddenly appeared and
sat by my bed and confirmed what I had
suspected - that the rest of my family
were missing, presumed dead - except of
course for my father who was away in the
R.A.F., and my much older brother Donald
who was doing something at Malvern that
he never talked about, even when we did
see him.

Auntie Lavender said that when I was
allowed to leave hospital I could go and live
with her at Thraxton permanently. I cried
with gratitude but also deep sadness that
I'd never see my mother or brother or
sister again. Sometimes, I was overwhelmed
with guilt that I'd let Sylvia go to the
outdoor privy because that was the last
thing she ever did, and I discovered later
that no trace of her was ever found. That
was the worst thing for me.

A nurse explained to Auntie how to
bandage the stump of my leg to keep it in
shape, and that was when I learned that
my leg had been 'amputated', and that I
was an 'amputee'. I'd never heard those
terms before.

I got to Auntie Lavender's house just
in time for Christmas that year, first on
a crowded train and then by pony and trap
from the station to Auntie's house. I
quickly made a lot of grown-up friends and

met some of the village children, all of
whom seemed to accept that I had only
one leg. It was not like the Christmases
I'd been used to.

'What happened to you?' people would
ask.

'I'm an amputee,' I replied proudly,
until someone explained that people really
wanted to know what had happened to
make me an amputee, after which I got
so used to telling my story that I became
heartily sick of it.

Auntie Lavender took me along to the
local school for the Spring Term. I was
a bit worried about having to go to school
on crutches, but I wasn't the only pupil
there who'd been injured or had something
wrong with them and, apart from a few
silly remarks, nobody took much notice
of me being different. One or two of my
classmates were especially kind and helpful
and became very good friends for life.
I still see them occasionally. Some of
the teachers were very helpful, and most
made allowances for those of us who took
longer than others to do things, which was
very surprising.

There was a gang of boys who I
found out were always competing to
catch a glimpse of the remains of my
leg, so I made sure that it was always
well protected by the special socks that
Auntie Lavender knitted for me from a

seemingly inexhaustible supply of thick green wool. I also wore a long skirt to hide my stump as it was a long time before it became acceptable for girls to wear trousers (rather later in rural Thraxton than in busy towns).

More than once, those boys thought it was a huge joke to spirit my crutches away and hide them. Most times, my best friend Honor Franklin (she's still my friend to this day) would go and find them for me, but if she wasn't around I had to hop or sometimes crawl about to find them for myself which caused the boys great amusement. I refused to be upset, because that only made them worse, and so do it more often.

There was a basketmaker in the village called Stanley Fisher who'd heard about me (it seemed everybody had) and he sent a message round to Auntie Lavender saying that he could make me an artificial leg if I would like and that it wouldn't cost very much because I was young and still at school and he wanted to help and make things easier for me. He'd made several artificial legs for wounded soldiers after the First World War.

So I went to see him, and he took some measurements, and found a short log the diameter of my stump from his special collection, which he would use to weave a socket for me. He also showed Auntie

Lavender how to bandage the stump of my leg in a particular way to help make it firm and compact, which would help with the leg.

When I went back to see him after a fortnight he showed me the leg he'd been making for me. He had wedged canes into a piece of stout bamboo, and had shaped the loose ends of the canes round the special log (which was now stored on a shelf with my name written on it), and had woven them into a basketwork tube for me to push the stump of my leg into.

I had to lie flat on my back, and Mr Fisher carefully measured the length the leg needed to be and cut a bit off the end - pushing on a little rubber ferrule like you'd have on the end of a walking stick. I found that with a bit of practice and one of my crutches to help balance I could soon walk on my new leg.

It was very crude, but it worked, and with the green stump socks Auntie Lavender knitted for me it was pretty comfortable and soon became part of me. Because the stump of my leg was quite long the false leg held on pretty firmly, but to make sure it stayed on I had a simple strap fastened to it that went over my left shoulder.

The early legs Mr Fisher made me were all in one piece, so they stuck out in front of me when I sat down, unless

I sat right on the edge of the seat so that the end of the leg could rest on the floor. If I wanted to avoid it sticking straight out, I could slip the leg off but I didn't always feel comfortable not wearing it. Later, Mr Fisher made me a leg with a knee hinge that could be released for sitting and locked for walking. Mr Fisher was my leg supplier until well after I'd finished growing and the National Health Service came into being and started to supply 'proper' legs - which was about the time he retired. Looking back on it, it could have been much worse.

So I spent my school years either on crutches, or with a crude - but effective - Fisher leg. I learnt to ride a bicycle with a toe-clip on the left pedal and the Fisher leg dangling, and I became pretty good on roller skates using a special Fisher leg with a roller skate attached to it. In the summer I loved to play tennis, hopping about on one leg, or using a crutch modified by Mr Fisher.

At one Harvest Supper after the War I met Lady Pamela Morris who had lost a leg in a motoring accident before the War, and we became great friends. She gave me the very special pair of rosewood crutches with maroon leather tops attached with brass studs which I keep polished up and ready for special occasions. In fact, I once met the

Queen on them several years ago. They were not adjustable, and Lady M had grown out of them. She was bigger than me but they were exactly my size so I was very glad to have them. I called them my Lady Ms. She found that highly amusing.

Seeing that I was interested, Lady M gave me several artificial legs and crutches, the start of my collection, which I hope will provide some historical interest somewhere, albeit somewhat specialist.

As soon as I left school, I went to work in a florist's shop called Winchester's, and after a couple of years I moved to another part of the firm - the nursery that supplied the shop, and many other retailers in the area. I eventually became the manager of what became known as one of the first Garden Centres in the area and after a few years married the boss - Harry Winchester.

We had two children - Kenneth and Sylvia (named in memory of my late siblings). Sylvia married Stuart Macey and they had a daughter - Lorna. When Harry died suddenly, Lorna came to live with me.

Now that I've retired, Kenneth and his sister run the business. And now my story is approaching the present, I'll leave my account for younger pens to continue.

I've had an exciting and eventful life and have enjoyed a wonderfully helpful and supportive family.

I hope that those who come after
will find this account interesting, and
that it will keep alive the memory of my
family and that unforgettable night of the
Moonlight Sonata air raid on Coventry.

Delia Winchester

'Wow!' said Hannah when she'd finished reading. 'Amazing.'

They decided to take the box back to Lorna, and witness her excitement at discovering more of her family's history.

⁂

Once she was alone again, Hannah went to the cupboard and pulled out the original leg that Stanley Fisher had made for Delia. As always when she held it, she felt curiously close to the girl injured during the War. She wondered whether the frisson it gave her was peculiar to her, as no one else would understand just how important it must have been to Delia, a young girl still trying to get over the loss of her family.

Hannah sat down and held the leg across her lap. She marvelled at the way in which Stanley Fisher had woven the socket from a bunch of canes wedged into a length of hollow bamboo, and added a rubber ferrule to its lower end. She tried all the parts of the leg for strength, suddenly convinced that she owed it to Delia to try the leg on.

She found that her stump fitted the socket when she pulled on two of Delia's knitted green stump socks. Then she lay flat on her bed and swivelled round to find that the artificial leg was of the right length.

Excitedly, she stood up carefully with her crutches to give her balance and threw the retaining strap over her shoulder. She made sure that it was properly fastened to the leg at each end; then, with a bit of trial and error she found she could actually walk on the leg that had given its original owner mobility more than seventy years earlier.

A quarter of an hour later, Hannah had pulled on a pair of fancy trousers and a spangly top and felt confident that this was an outfit in which she could appear in public – when she was ready.

# 12

## Polly Trembath

Desperate to get out more and talk to people other than her family, Hannah decided to go for a walk, just up to the shop. Her clothes were crucial to her self-esteem and she decided on her denim trousers.

She stood up after breakfast: 'I'm going out for a walk ... by myself ...'

'Keep still ... umm ... do you want me to come with you? ... or to follow at a discreet distance? ... or anything?' asked Frankie, arranging the leg of Hannah's trousers without being asked, and still worried about the attack.

'No, I don't think so, thanks very much. I won't go far. Just up to Mrs Belbin's, so that I'll be bound to meet a few people ... I just want to ... umm ... see how it goes.'

❧

Up leafy Arboretum Avenue (mind the slippery leaves); hardly a soul. She turned into Trafalgar Road, where she met a little old lady with a dog, and ventured: 'That's a fine dog ... Oh! Hello, Mrs Taylor.'

Mrs Taylor looked at her. 'Hello, dear. Hannah, isn't it? Oh dear, oh dear. What's happened to your leg?'

'I had an accident on my bike ...'

But Mrs Taylor had retreated into her shell, rather embarrassed because her fine dog was making a mess on the pavement and she had no means of picking it up.

❧

Hannah's next encounter was with a telephone engineer sitting on an upturned bucket in front of a large roadside box with its doors wide open and a tangle of multicoloured wires spilling out: 'Oooh! That looks complicated. How do you know which wire goes where?'

'Well,' said the engineer, somewhat taken aback to be spoken to, 'I've got this book 'ere, you see. And they're all colour coded. You soon get used to how it is.'

'I know what you mean,' said Hannah, hiding a grin, 'you just *have* to get used to how it is, don't you …?'

Hannah continued on her way, storing up the details of her O-L début in the big wide world to take home with her, wondering what might happen next. It wasn't long before she met a girl about her own age, pushing a hi-tech pushchair with chunky wheels: 'That's a great pushchair … and a lovely little girl … what's her name?'

'I'm Polly,' said the little girl looking up at Hannah. 'I'm four, and where's your leg?'

'Polly!' reprimanded her mother.

'No, that's all right,' reassured Hannah; she turned to Polly: 'I had an altercation with a lorry, and …'

'What's an al-ter-cation?' asked Polly.

'Umm … well, sometimes it can be when your leg gets in the way of a lorry …'

'Can I have some sweeties mummy?'

'Wait and see what they've got.' The girl turned to Hannah: 'I'm Felicity, by the way. They call me Flick.'

'And I'm Hannah. Are we both going in here?'

They'd reached Mrs Belbin's, one of the few surviving old-fashioned corner shops in Frimley. As Hannah pushed open the door, there was the familiar sound of the slightly cracked bell.

She held the door open for Flick and the pushchair, then swung in, negotiating the narrow spaces between sacks and bins on the floor, boxes of as-yet-unpacked goods, and the motley collection of shelving (Mr Belbin's life's work), to make her way to the old-fashioned bentwood chair beside the counter.

Mrs Belbin welcomed Hannah with a tear in her eye: 'Hello Hannah; oh ... poor you! I heard you'd had a bad accident, and that must be as bad as it comes, losing a leg like that. Well, I suppose it might have been both legs. Perhaps an arm or two as well. Or you could have ... Listen to me burbling on ... So, how are you?'

'I'm good,' said Hannah, lowering herself on to the chair and laying her ocelots out of the way on the floor alongside the counter to talk. 'I sometimes think about what you say – that it might've been worse. A lot worse. Or I might be dead. As it is, here I am, and I'm jolly glad to be alive I can tell you. I'd like some strawberry jam and peanut butter. Please.'

Mrs Belbin fetched the jars: 'Anything else I can get you, dear?'

Hannah fished out her scribbled list: 'Ginger biscuits ...'

Mrs B moved around, her arms flailing, collecting the goods.

A young man in a sharp suit and shiny shoes appeared at the door. As he approached the counter, he noticed Hannah seated on the chair, did a double take, and burst out laughing: 'Hahaha ... excuse me ... the way you're sitting makes it look as though you've only got one leg.'

Hannah eyed the young sales rep nonplussed: 'Does it really? How odd ...'

At that moment, Mrs Belbin's young granddaughter Chloë came bouncing in and took in the scene: 'It's Hannah! Hi Hannah – how are you ... I heard you'd had a terrible accident, but here you are ... poor you, losing your leg like that! Does it hurt?'

'Hi, Chlo ... sometimes, yes ... now and again ... it's as under control as it can be.'

'And when do you get your new leg?'

'Ah ... people keep asking me that ... no, I'm happy on my crutches for the time being ...'

The sales rep became more and more uncomfortable until Mrs Belbin said: 'Sorry to keep you dear. Hannah here's an old friend. She's had a terrible accident as you can see. So what can I get for you today, dear?'

'Oh ... a couple of those hot pasties, please. I take it they're genuine Cornish? And a small jar of mustard. French. And two cans of that orange.' His purchases completed, the rep sidled out murmuring: 'Sorry' to Hannah, and standing to one side to avoid the girl with the great pushchair. Hannah hid her nervous laughter, unsure of how to further their conversation, though Chloë seemed to have it under control, bouncing forward: 'Hi Flick. How's Polly? Bit snuffly last time I saw you.'

'That was ages ago. She's fine now, thank goodness. Will you look after her while I go round the shop?'

Felicity looked sideways at Hannah: 'Do you know Hannah here?' asked Chloë. 'This is Felicity, known as Flick. She lives with her granny, cos her mum threw her out when she had Polly. And that's Polly.'

'We just met down the road,' said Hannah. 'Where does your gran live?'

'Cranford Road, just round the corner,' said Felicity. 'Tell you what, why don't you both come round for tea when I've finished shopping? Granny's cake is something else.'

§

Hannah and Flick had been talking like old friends for well over an hour, with hardly a mention of her missing leg. She made a suitable 'must go' noise, and reached for her crutches.

'Sorry you've got to go,' said Flick. 'Would you like to babysit for me sometime?'

'Umm … why not?' said Hannah, surprised that someone missing a leg should be asked to babysit – *and* after such a short acquaintance: 'Any particular idea when?'

'I've got to go over to Bramwall Campus the Thursday after next,' said Flick, 'to find out about the art course I'm thinking of going on.'

'Glad to be able to help,' said Hannah, surprised at herself. 'What sort of time?'

'I'll be going down the road to catch a coach at 9.45. And I should be back by 4 o'clock.'

'OK, but I think I'd better spend some time with Polly before then.'

With some trepidation, Hannah agreed to return at 10 o'clock on the following Monday.

On Monday morning, Jill dropped Hannah off at 37 Cranford Road on her way to Frimley.

Flick opened the door to find Hannah on her Lady Ms, wearing an owl print top and her favourite blue denim trousers.

Polly appeared as a fairy, grinning, with a tiara and an elaborate wand with sparkly lights. Hannah stood her Lady Ms out of the way, hopped over to Polly, and with some difficulty knelt down to her level: 'That's a great wand,' she said.

'My mummy bought it at the fair,' said Polly. 'Would you like to see my dolls' house? My daddy made it for me in his workshop.'

'Yes please,' said Hannah. 'Do you mind?' she asked Flick, who shook her head.

With one of the Lady Ms as a hoppy, Hannah followed Polly upstairs and into her room, where a large wooden dolls' house stood by the wall. She grabbed a chair next to it so that Polly could show her all the furniture.

But Polly had already moved on and brought out a huge doll instead: 'This is Milly,' she said. 'I had her for my birthday last month.'

Hannah remembered her first doll; Milly was so like Henrietta: 'Wow, Polly,' she said, 'she's nearly as big as you – maybe even bigger.'

'Yes, but *I'll* grow,' said Polly.

'And how old were you on your birthday?'

'I was four. Milly's wearing a pair of my pyjamas – she likes the animals.' Polly followed Hannah back downstairs, holding Milly: 'Can't leave her upstairs on her own.' Hannah found Flick in the garden under a sunshade. Chatting to Flick with one eye on Polly, seldom had Hannah felt so comfortable outside the family in recent weeks.

Jill arrived, ostensibly to pick Hannah up, but more to satisfy her curiosity about Flick and Polly, and ensure that Hannah could cope when Flick visited the Bramwall Campus. Secretly, Hannah wished her mum would let her make her own decisions – she was an adult, after all.

❧

Flick rang Hannah later: 'I must say, Polly's fallen for you in a big way.'

'How's that?' asked Hannah.

'You'll see when you come,' said Flick mysteriously, before hanging up.

Returning to Cranford Road on the Thursday, Hannah felt more confident about taking her single 'Lady M'. Flick told her everything she needed to know.

Suddenly there was a 'thump thump thump' on the stairs, and Polly appeared dragging Milly. Hannah's heart missed a few beats when she saw that Milly now had only one leg.

'Here's Hoppy-Poppy,' announced Polly. 'Look – she's only got one leg now. Like you.'

'So she has,' said Hannah, trying to look unperturbed. 'What's her new name?'

'Hoppy-Poppy,' replied Polly. 'She doesn't have sticks like you. She hops.'

Hannah stretched out to take Hoppy-Poppy and noted that Polly had folded up Milly's leg inside the pyjama trousers.

'I thought she was called Milly,' said Flick quietly and dryly.

'Well, now she's Hoppy-Poppy,' said Polly firmly, sitting her on a nearby chair.

'Right,' said Flick, 'I'm off now, so you be a good girl and have a nice day. And thanks again, Hannah, for coming in. I'll see you later.'

'Shall we sit in the garden and have something to drink?' asked Hannah of her new four-year-old friend..

'Yes,' said Polly, 'and you can read to me. Of course, I *can* read … nearly.'

Minutes later, they were sitting cosily on the swing seat, with Hoppy-Poppy between them. Polly was drinking in little sips from a pink tumbler, as Hannah read about the snail and the butterfly.

'Hannah,' said Polly, 'where can I get a stick like yours for Hoppy-Poppy?'

Hannah thought: 'Well,' she said carefully, 'it's called a crutch. Why does she want one?'

'She's tired of hopping,' said Polly. 'Now she's seen you, she wants a … cwutch.'

'I could see if I could get one for you. For next time.'

'It's for *her*,' said Polly. 'Get one for her, please. Why don't you have two legs?'

Hannah had been sure that Polly would ask sooner or later: 'Well …' Hannah measured her words carefully, 'my left leg was damaged by a lorry, so the doctor thought it would be better if I didn't have it any more.'

'Oh! Did you once have two legs, then?'

Would this give Polly bad dreams, Hannah wondered, before continuing her tale: 'Yes ... this is my right leg ... [she patted it] ... but the left leg was hurt, you see, so the doctor said it'd be better if it wasn't there any more, and I went to sleep, and when I woke up he'd ... taken it away. And then everything was much better.'

'What did he do with it when he'd taken it away? Is he going to put it back?'

Hannah hesitated; then she found the answer: 'Do you know, I haven't talked to him about that. But I don't miss it. That's the good part about it. Now, what about this story?'

'Can I see the place where the doctor took your leg away from?'

'No,' said Hannah firmly, 'that's very private. But I'll tell you what ... I'll let you see it if he puts my leg back. Now, I really do think we ought to get on with your story, otherwise it'll be lunch-time.'

'Do you think *I* could have one leg?'

Hannah had a sudden panic that she might be 'infecting' Polly with the idea of having one leg. What should she do? She had never dealt with this situation before. Had anyone? Polly had acquired an O-L babysitter who hopped, or walked with a crutch, and now she'd also got an O-L doll wanting a crutch. All Hannah could do was to carry on calmly and naturally: 'I think you're better as you are. You can run about, go on your scooter, ride your bicycle, bounce on the trampoline and everything. You should enjoy having two legs, that's best.'

'But you said you didn't miss your leg; you said not having it was a good thing.'

This was getting very difficult: 'Yes, well, I said that it was a good thing that I didn't miss my leg, not that it was a good thing not to have it. Now, I really think we ought to have this story ...'

'But it must be good that you don't have your leg if it was hurt.'

Hannah felt herself breaking into a sweat. Babysitting wasn't as simple as she'd hoped: 'Well, of course that's right, but it would have been better if it hadn't been hurt in the first place.'

At last, Hannah finished the story and managed to persuade Polly to follow her into the kitchen to get lunch. Together they carried everything into the dining-room, with Polly watching Hannah's every move.

After lunch, Polly tried to carry the dishes back to the kitchen in the way she'd seen Hannah carry them, trying to hop at the same time. It took Hannah some time to get Polly to her room for her afternoon rest. The rest was a short one. In no time, there was a 'bump, bump, bump' on the stairs as Polly came back down with Hoppy-Poppy.

'Now, if I'm going to get Hoppy-Poppy a crutch, I need to measure how long it should be,' said Hannah, seeking ways to distract Polly. 'Have you a tape-measure?'

'Mummy's got one in her sewing-basket,' said Polly. 'I'll get it.'

She went into the other room. There was a crash, a silence, and a wail. Hannah leapt up and hopped through to find the sewing-basket upside-down and its contents all over the floor:

'Oh ... dear,' she said. 'We'd better clear all this up. But – look – there's the tape-measure.'

Clearing up on one leg was quite a challenge; luckily, Polly was occupied with the tape-measure, and didn't make it any harder for her.

No sooner had Hannah made a note of Hoppy-Poppy's measurements, than Polly wanted to go back into the garden – still she watched in fascination every move that Hannah made.

Just as Hannah felt she'd successfully looked after Polly without incident for the day, Flick phoned to say she'd missed the coach – could Hannah stay another hour or so and give Polly her tea and settle her upstairs. Polly was overjoyed; Hannah less so. After tea, Polly carried Hoppy-Poppy upstairs: 'She's going to come into bed with me, and I can tell her all about you and how you have one leg like her, and how you're going to get her a cwutch so that she won't have to hop any more. And I can tell her about you having one leg because the doctor thought you'd be better that way …'

Hannah went cold, and having settled Polly, she went downstairs still somewhat shaken. She could hear the girl talking away to her doll, but after a while the sound tailed off and there was silence. The longer Hannah thought about it, the more she worried that she might have had a terrible long-term effect on Polly. What would Flick say?

෪

At last Flick returned, full of enthusiasm about the course. She'd decided to enrol on it and wanted only to hear that Polly had been no trouble. '… but I'm afraid we dropped your sewing-basket so it might be a bit higgledy-piggledy …' confessed Hannah.

'Er … that's OK. What did you need that for?'

Hannah wished she hadn't mentioned it, but then thought that at some point Polly would probably let the cat out of the bag anyway: 'Oh … Polly wanted me to get her a "cwutch" for her doll Hoppy-Poppy – or Milly – so I needed to measure her … Milly, that is.'

'Ah, that's very good of you. She didn't say anything to me about your … leg, but I think she was mightily impressed by your having one leg, and she soon converted her doll. I do hope you don't mind; I thought it better not to say anything to her. I hope you're not … embarrassed.'

'No, not at all. I think she was naturally … curious. Some people are. I think it's best to take it in your stride, as you might say. I hope *you're* OK with it …' They continued like this for some time.

※

Frankie was fascinated to hear about the day with Polly, and the birth of Hoppy-Poppy, and the fact that Hannah had said she was going to get her a crutch.

'She'll need a pair of crutches, and they'll have to be good and solid …'

'Why's that?'

'Knowing Polly, I wouldn't be surprised if she wanted to use them herself, so she'd better have two rather than one. I don't want to be responsible for her being injured.'

'There's a lovely pair of child's crutches in Delia's Hoard,' remembered Frankie.

'So there is. It'll be great for them to be used properly.'

※

A few days later, Hannah took the child's crutches round to Flick's. Polly brought Hoppy-Poppy downstairs in great excitement. Hannah stood her on the crutches and, surprisingly found that they were a perfect length: 'There you are,' she said, 'I've brought her a pair, rather than just the one, so that she'll stand up better. You see? You can lean her forward, and a leg and two crutches make a triangle. Very stable.'

Hannah set up Hoppy-Poppy, and her heart missed a beat when she saw just how suitable the crutches would be for Polly, but she didn't say anything and hoped that Polly didn't notice.

'Those are lovely,' said Flick. 'Very clever. And kind. Surely you didn't make them yourself? Do I owe you anything?'

'Nothing, that's fine,' said Hannah. 'But I would like them back when Polly's finished with them.' She reddened: 'Or should I say, when Hoppy-Poppy's finished with them?' And to Polly: 'Is Hoppy-Poppy coming out into the garden with us?'

'OK,' said Polly, and rushed on ahead of them.

Hannah and Flick sat under the sunshade chatting, while Polly played with Hoppy-Poppy; then, after a sidelong glance at her mum, started to experiment with the crutches herself. Hannah pretended not to notice.

ॐ

A week or two later, Flick invited Hannah round again.

They were sitting in the garden when suddenly Polly appeared with her left leg bent up inside her pyjama trousers like Hoppy-Poppy, walking competently on Hoppy-Poppy's crutches. Hannah's heart stopped momentarily – what *had* she done?

'Oh Polly,' said Hannah, 'What *are* you doing?'

'Hoppy-Poppy lent me her cwutches,' said Polly. 'I need them to get about, now I've only got one leg. You see?'

She demonstrated her prowess: 'I'm pwactising because I'm going to ask the doctor if he'll take my leg away, like he did yours,' she said to Hannah.

'I don't think you should do that,' said Hannah, her heart skipping a beat. 'I can assure you that life's a lot easier with two legs.'

'Yes, but I don't need two legs now I've got the cwutches,' said Polly. 'Anyway, *you* get along fine.'

Hannah felt hot and cold.

'It's time for us to go and get an ice-cream now,' said Flick, changing the subject swiftly. 'Don't want to miss that, Polly, do you? Please go and get ready.'

Noisily, Polly crutched away to her room.

Suddenly there was a massive thump and a loud cry. 'What's happened?' shouted Flick, running upstairs.

There was no response, and she found Polly rubbing her head with a bruise developing even as she sat on the floor in a daze.

'Now I'll give these cwutches back to Hoppy-Poppy, and we can go and get some ice-cream,' said Polly.

'You can tell me which is your favourite flavour,' said Hannah, hoping that Polly wouldn't be playing with the crutches again, and that Hoppy-Poppy would become their sole owner.

# 13

## Petra Hardy

Hannah and Frankie sat in the waiting room at the Artificial Limb Centre, next to a young girl wearing a floral top with medium-length frilly sleeves and a flimsy scarf draped over her left shoulder.

'Quite a nice day today? When I come here, it's usually raining.'

'Is it really? ... And do you come here a lot?' asked Hannah, unsure of the girl's situation.

'I've been coming in a bit recently because they want me to try a new design of arm. It's made of carbon fibre and activated by myoelectric electrodes. I think about what I want it to do, and it does it. That's the theory. Clever, or what?'

'Certainly is ...' Hannah was no longer surprised when strangers started telling her all their medical details. There was a pause. 'I'm Hannah and this is my sister Frankie.'

'And I'm Petra.'

Hannah looked at Petra more closely, and saw that her left arm stopped above where she would have had an elbow: 'I'd never have noticed you were missing a bit of an arm,' she said, amazed.

'Ah ... that's why I always say it's better to be missing an arm than a leg. More easily disguised. If that's what you want, of course.'

'Well ... I'm not sure that ... it's always necessary to disguise ...'

'How do you disguise your missing leg? What about the crutches? 'Spose you were in a wheelchair?'

'I could be in a wheelchair, with a rug over my knee, but I'd hate that,' said Hannah. 'But I haven't tried it – yet. To tell the truth, I'm not too bothered.'

'Hmm ... And in case you're wondering, I was born this way.'

'Umm ... And I've only been this way for a few weeks ...'

'Awww. So you're being fitted for your first leg?'

'Yes. This is my second fitting, working towards the real thing … [And to tell you the truth, thought Hannah, I'm not very impressed] … But losing – missing – an arm must be … [Hannah thought of all the things she needed both arms for and shuddered] … Well, if I had to lose something, I think I'd rather lose a leg.'

'Whatever,' said Petra. 'I've never had a proper left arm, just shorty, so I don't know. You have to use a wheelchair or crutches or something to get about, don't you? I just wear my scarf. I'm right handed, so not having a left hand is no big deal. And what I've never had …'

'Do you always wear a scarf like that? It's a great idea,' said Hannah.

'Something an old one-armed lady told me about years ago. Went to our Prom a while ago, with a lovely dress, and a scarf arranged to hang down like this, and lots of people didn't even notice.'

'How did you know?'

'Oh! I can tell when they suddenly spot it. You can see it in their eyes. You soon work that one out.'

'That's true,' said Hannah. 'It's like a …'

'So what's this myoelectric thing?' asked Frankie, changing the subject abruptly.

'Well, there's areas on the skin around the end of shorty – my short arm – where I can generate an electric current just by thinking about flexing various muscles – that's what myoelectric means: electric currents generated by muscles. Then the currents are picked up by electrodes. So they have this socket with contacts that they plug on to shorty, and then the little currents open and close your grip, turn your hand, move your fingers, all that sort of thing. The arm's got little motors inside it. It's the batteries that weigh, but of course they can be remote from the arm itself. And if the connections are taken from me to the pros on the bench, I can make a disembodied hand do things just by thinking about it. Spooky.'

'Have you had an artificial arm before?' asked Frankie, overcome with curiosity.

'To tell the truth, yes and no,' said Petra. 'When you're little, everyone seems to think that, because *they* have two arms, you must feel short of an arm. But of course you don't, because that's how you are. So your family notices you're "different", and thinks that you ought to be made to look "normal". After all, they're not used to the idea of having a child with one arm. So they give you an artificial arm. I found it annoying, so I didn't use it very much, and I often used to lose it around the place on purpose – until my parents got the message. I think it was more important for them than for me.'

'I think it's like that with the leg I haven't got yet,' said Hannah. 'It's more that other people think I should look "normal" than that I want it. In fact, I quite like my crutches – absolutely no pain involved … but we'll see. Silly not to find out what it's like if you get the chance.'

'Yeah. So when I went to nursery school, I had a body-powered arm: it's a special sort of split hook plugged on to the end of shorty, with an artificial elbow I could adjust with my other hand, and a harness round my shoulder so that I could open and close the split hook by shrugging. It wasn't a crude hook like Captain Hook's hook, but it's called a "split hook" and you can open and close it, which gives you a bit of control over things. I wore it a lot cos most everybody else thought it was fun and that made me feel good.'

'And then what?'

'When I moved to secondary school I gave it up. It wasn't terribly useful, cos if you've got one arm, that's what you use for doing things. If I'm wearing a jacket, I keep the end of my sleeve in my pocket, and I can still hold things under shorty if I want. I've also got a cosmetic arm now, which I don't put on very often but it can save a lot of awkwardness if I'm meeting new people. And I could have an adult split hook like the one I had at nursery school, but I don't want one really, and now there's this new myoelectric arm thing they think I ought to try. It'll probably end up in my cupboard, but it wouldn't be fair not to give it a go. Especially when such a lot of work has gone into it.'

'I see your point,' said Hannah. 'But can it do things you can't do now? What can't you do now, anyway?'

'Wringing out wet clothes, opening some jars, clapping ... I don't put up my hair up very often, and there are quite a lot of musical instruments I can't play. And, of course, I can't throw both arms round someone. But why try to do what you can't? And if I *do* want to do something, I can usually ask someone for help. It must be the same for you if you can't do something.'

'Yes, I suppose it is. I haven't spent a lot of time moaning about the things I can't do any more since I lost my leg.'

'Did you lose your leg recently, then?'

'Yes, only a few weeks ago. I was on my bicycle, and I was run over by a lorry.'

'Wow! That's not very funny. But I suppose they'll plug a leg on to you soon?'

'They're working on it.'

At that moment Petra was called, and they wished each other 'good luck' as she went off. 'That was an interesting girl,' said Frankie. 'What a conversation!'

# 14

## John Macpherson

annah had an appointment the following Wednesday to see Dr Peters, followed by Mr Macpherson, to make a start on her new leg. As the day approached she wondered how she would feel about walking again – should she be nervous and excited?

It so happened that both Frankie and Olivia were around that day, and offered to accompany Hannah to share all the new information that would doubtless be coming her way.

❧

Olivia drove, and at the last moment Hannah asked Frankie to push her to the appointment in her wheelchair. She still preferred her crutches but had found that sometimes the wheelchair wasn't as bad as she had thought. As they were all sitting in the rehab waiting area by Dr Peters's office, along came a health-care assistant accompanying a man with no arms. Hannah found herself thinking how trivial was her own loss compared with his; discussing the incident later, they found that they had all felt oddly embarrassed. He eyed them up and down with a relaxed smile; they found themselves smiling and nodding back at him, their own arms seemingly paralysed.

'Hannah Brooks! May we have Hannah Brooks please?!' Beaming Nurse Lois waited by Dr Peters's open door, and they made their way into the room, Frankie pushing Hannah's wheelchair.

Dr Peters shook hands with them as they positioned themselves: 'OK; sit down, sit down, make yourselves comfortable. Now, first of all, Hannah and …?'

'... I'm Hannah's older sister Olivia ...'

'... and I'm her younger sister Frankie ...'

'... and we thought that it would be a good thing if we *all* came to hear what you've got to say,' said Hannah, by way of explanation.

'Good idea, especially if you're a very close family, as you obviously are. Now, I'm Dr Brian Peters, Jimmy's Consultant in Rehabilitation, and I specialise in prosthetics and orthotics. That means I'm the one who assesses people's needs – and in this case guides them to the appropriate prosthetic limbs.'

There was a pause. Dr Peters inspected an X-ray of Hannah's stump on his screen, zooming in and out and here and there. Then: 'Right, Hannah ... let's have a look.'

Hannah wheeled forward, and Nurse Lois removed her shrinker so that Dr Peters could examine her more closely: 'Interesting stump. How active were you before the accident?'

Hannah told him about her swimming and diving, and Dr Peters nodded and made notes. Then he quizzed her on her medication, and her experience of pain, examined her again, and concluded that for the moment a leg with a temporary socket would be best suited to her, until her stump – still healing – had settled down further. 'We'll need to make you a new socket in due course,' he explained, 'but we can use the other parts of the leg again.'

He scribbled a few notes on Hannah's file, and then sent the sisters straight to the next appointment – with John Macpherson, the prosthetist who'd be looking after Hannah.

'Mr Mac's a very gentle man,' said Rosemary, his assistant, and he's been making legs for me for nearly ten years. Absolutely first class.'

'What?' asked Hannah, looking curiously at Rosemary's legs, and noting that the right one appeared to be made of plastic and metal.

'What happened to you then?'

'I had a bicycle accident when I was fourteen,' said Rosemary, 'and lost my right leg below the knee.'

'I had a bicycle accident when I was nineteen,' said Hannah, 'and lost my left leg above the knee.'

'Umm … There's a difference, you know,' said Rosemary, matter-of-factly. 'BK and AK make very different demands on the patient. And on the prosthetist.'

Once he'd guided them to his room, and introductions were complete, Mr Macpherson ('call me Mac') lost no time in getting down to business. He barely glanced at the file from Dr Peters that Rosemary had laid upon his desk: 'Right … well, let's have a closer look at your stump then, Hannah,' he said, sizing her up. 'Ooh! … That looks … interesting. The wound's healing well, but there's still some way to go, and there's some slight oedema – swelling – just here, in spite of your shrinker. Anyway, yes, you're not in bad shape, and we can certainly start the process of making you a new leg.'

'That's great to hear …' interrupted Hannah.

'First, though … I just need to check that you'll be able to use the leg when you *do* get it – though I don't see why you shouldn't … so will you please just walk down there and back for me?'

'Yeah, sure …' Hannah pushed herself up as Olivia passed her her ocelots from the caddy on the back of the chair, and she crutched across the room and back to Mac.

'OK … you can sit down again … I've seen enough. You're obviously strong, your body control's excellent, your balance is good; everything's OK for the moment …'

'Great news!'

'… but I ought to say that me providing the prosthesis and getting it right is one thing; you being able to use it is another. You'll have to get used to how your stump behaves throughout the day, how to save energy, how to walk naturally – but Dolores and her team will help you through all that later.'

'How do you mean, about my "getting used to how my stump behaves throughout the day"?' queried Hannah, confused.

'Well, your stump will change shape throughout the day, and the size of the socket of your leg is fixed, so you'll have to alter the thickness of socks you wear between the stump of your leg and the socket. It sounds complicated, but you'll soon get used to it.'

'The socket is what fastens the prosthesis to Hannah's stump?' asked Olivia.

'Well, it doesn't so much fasten it as provide an interface,' said Mac, 'but yes: it's what fits on to the stump.'

'And how long will my first leg last?' asked Hannah.

'Well,' said Mac, 'you'll probably have more than one socket as your stump gradually settles down to its final shape … we'll start with a belt round your middle fastened with Velcro, on a "beginner's socket" – easy to cut about and re-shape when we want to work on it. When we can no longer adjust the fit by adding or subtracting socks, we make a new socket.'

'And then?' asked Hannah, beginning to suspect that things might not be as easy as she'd imagined, or as she'd been given to believe.

'We'll have to see. We have to follow the conventional path, certainly for the moment.'

Olivia and Frankie were soaking up all the new things that Hannah would have to remember, and were mindful of how useful it was that they were present at this session.

'I'm glad to know that,' said Hannah, storing the information away. 'But how long will the leg last me when we've got it right?'

'It should go on for at least a couple of years. You should be fine … with kids we usually have to modify and adjust their prostheses quite frequently because they grow so quickly.'

'Umm … I think I've done all my growing for now,' said Hannah.

Mac wasn't going to waste any time: 'Right, so, first of all, I need to make a cast of your stump using plaster of Paris bandages, so I want you to slip off your shorts and come and stand between the parallel bars here while I set up a casting jig with a cuff the right size for your stump.'

'A jig? You want me to dance?'

'Hold your horses ...'

Mac set up a jig on the floor and then set up a cuff of the right diameter for Hannah's stump on the jig so that Hannah could stand comfortably and push her stump into position.

Then as she stood there, he protected the surface of her stump by applying a thin plastic wrap, soaked some plaster bandages in water, and applied them to Hannah – not too tight, not too loose.

'There – I've finished the cast,' said Mac. 'Does it feel OK?'

'Yes ... it's quite warm.'

'Ah, the setting process generates heat you see ... Now we let the plaster harden a bit before you pull out; then you can dress again and you're free to go after Rosemary has sorted out an appointment for you to come back in a couple of weeks.'

'Cool.'

'OK – now it's time to pull your stump out of the mould – it should be easy because of the plastic wrap.' Mac steadied the hardware, Hannah pulled a little, and sure enough out came her stump.

'There we are,' said Mac. 'When it's properly hardened, this mould is filled with a plaster mixture to make a positive cast of your stump for working on.'

'OK ... So there'll be a plaster model of my stump to help you make the socket to fit on to it?'

'That's it. I'm glad to say your stump's slightly tapered, even though the end is somewhat uneven, and so it should – *should* – just slip in to the socket.'

'Ooh ... it all feels quite cold now,' said Hannah, giggling at the unusual sensation.

'So it will,' said Mac. 'Anyway, that's you done for today. But don't forget – we'll have to go through this process again as your stump settles down to its final shape – no doubt more than once.'

Olivia helped Hannah back on with her shrinker and shorts, and she wheeled out of the room to see Rosemary to make her next appointment with Mac, relieved the session was over.

Olivia wouldn't be able to accompany Hannah to her next session, but Frankie was free. 'Don't forget to bring your matching shoe,' reminded Rosemary.

Then they made their way to the tea-room. Frankie and Olivia went to the counter to buy some refreshment while Hannah parked her wheelchair out of the way, and made her way to the table on her crutches, preferring to sit in a 'normal' chair.

She had just found a convenient place to park her ocelots when she heard a voice: 'Hi Hannah, good to see you. How are you getting along? How's the leg?' It was Ben, who came and sat down at the table without being invited.

'I've just had my first session at the prosthetic clinic,' said Hannah, wondering why Ben was there.

'Getting there, then,' said Ben. He sat and looked her in the eye for a long time, saying nothing. At last: 'Tracy keeps saying she's really sorry she attacked you like that,' he said.

'It's a really good thing that I found out who she was and why – however strange the explanation. If I *hadn't* found out, I'd be scared stiff to go out of doors now.'

'Umm … it was … awful,' said Ben, 'but I'm glad it's sorted. I'm here for a stoma clinic. Haven't seen you for ages. How long before you're up on two feet?'

'I've just been to my first leg clinic,' Hannah said. 'Not long to go now. Just two weeks it seems, and I'll be walking on two feet again.' For all her doubts, she now had a rosy expectation of walking again when she got the leg.

'Wow! Good luck. I must be off now …' Ben touched the top

of her head and darted off to his clinic, at the sight of his mum gesturing impatiently.

೫೦

Hannah closed her eyes and imagined walking on two legs. She was so completely used to her crutches and, to a certain extent, her wheelchair, that she could scarcely recall what it felt like to have two legs. She realised that when she got her new leg, it'd be an extension of her stump that she could walk on, but as she'd be sitting on the edge of her socket, she wouldn't be able to feel anything beyond the end of her stump. So how would she learn to know where her fake foot was?

Hannah tried to explain what she was thinking, but she could see that her audience wasn't entirely clear what she was talking about, though the frowns showed that they were trying hard, and eventually she dropped the topic.

೫೦

'Wakey, wakey, Hannah'

'What …?'

'It's your leg day, remember?'

'How could I forget … is the bathroom free?'

'Yep … Oli's just come out.'

Hannah swung out of bed and hopped to the bathroom with a crutch to steady her, thinking that if all went well she'd be able to walk there tomorrow on her own … two feet. She took longer than usual, making sure that her stump was in good order, properly clean and patted dry, examining it carefully all round the end with a mirror she'd earmarked for the purpose, still unsure of what she thought about it.

Back in her room, she donned her shrinker, dressed in her

best leg-collecting shorts and a woolly top, and descended for breakfast: 'Well, guys, this is it …'

'Yeah … hope it all goes according to plan.'

Frankie finished breakfast, made sure Hannah's bag contained the matching left shoe, and told her she was ready to go to Jimmy's. Hannah decided to use her crutches and on arrival at the Rehab entrance, she swung in for her appointment, as Frankie went to park.

Hannah was met by Mac: 'Ah, Hannah, wonderful timing, come on through. I hope you're looking forward to what we've got for you today.'

Now that the moment had come Hannah felt quite light-headed, and didn't know what to think: 'Is it ready?'

'Of course … would you like to take off your shorts and shrinker and sit there while I fetch it?' Mac went to fetch Hannah's leg, and returned holding it triumphantly.

'Wowee! It looks enormous,' said Hannah in surprise. 'Well, enormouser than you'd think it would.'

'People often think that when they first see a prosthesis,' said Mac. Hannah reached out and took hold of the leg: 'Wow!' she said. 'I didn't realise it'd weigh *this* much.' She examined the prosthesis closely, trying to disguise her surprise and disappointment at what she was seeing.

Frankie arrived from parking and saw the leg. 'Is that it?' she exclaimed.

'And just you try the weight,' sniffed Hannah, passing Frankie the leg.

'Stone the crows,' said Frankie slightly embarrassedly.

'OK, OK,' said Mac, slightly testily. 'I hope you've remembered to bring the matching left shoe.'

'How could I let her forget that?' asked Frankie. She passed the shoe to Mac, who retrieved the leg, snuggled the shoe on to its foot and passed it back to Hannah.

'Moment of truth,' he said. 'Would you lift your stump up for me, please?' Mac produced a white stump sock and smoothed it on to Hannah's stump. 'The idea is that as your stump changes shape throughout the day – as it will – you adjust the thickness of the socks you're wearing to maintain the fit, because of course the socket of the leg doesn't change shape. Now push yourself into the socket and see how it feels.'

Hannah stood up between the parallel bars and with Mac's help eased and pushed her stump into the socket until she thought she could feel it was where it ought to be. Mac pulled the retaining belt round her and Velcroed it snugly.

'How's that then?' he asked.

'I don't know,' said Hannah, 'I've no idea what it *ought* to feel like. All I can say is, the leg weighs a ton, and it digs in a bit here, and even worse here.' She indicated where the discomfort had appeared.

'Only to be expected on a first outing,' said Mac knowledgably. He made a note of the problem areas, pulled the leg off, and retired to his workshop.

⌘

While Mac was away at his bench adjusting the leg, Hannah and Frankie took stock of the situation.

'It really does weigh a ton,' said Hannah quietly. 'I had no idea it would be like it is. I must admit I thought it would just slip on and I'd be walking. People always seem to give the impression that they'll "fix me up with a new leg" and "I'll be as good as new". There ought to be a law against making everything look like it's all going to get sorted – and quickly.'

Frankie felt angry; she felt oddly let down on her sister's behalf. They'd both set out that morning with high hopes and now, comparing notes, they felt as if they'd been dropped into a vat of cold porridge.

Mac reappeared with the adjusted leg; Hannah glanced at her watch to find that he'd been away nearly an hour, and that they hadn't really noticed the passage of time.

'Try this,' he said with a smile, confident that it would be an improvement.

Hannah stood between the parallel bars and once again tried to don the leg. At last: 'There!' she said when she thought she'd succeeded. With some difficulty she took a few faltering steps, only to find that the painful areas around her stump had moved to different places.

At the same time, Mac saw another slight adjustment to be made to the angle of the ankle, and was down on the floor with his Allen key; then asking Hannah to doff the leg again so that he could bear it away to his workshop for another adjustment session.

'I'm not sure that I can take much more of this,' confided Hannah to Frankie when Mac had gone.

'It really doesn't look at all … comfortable,' said Frankie, wanting to be helpful and supportive, at the same time sympathising that Hannah seemed to be getting a raw deal. 'Perhaps things will improve as time goes on.'

༄

At last Mac returned with the leg for Hannah to try it again. Once more she worked it on to her stump, and once more she had no idea whether or not it was in its correct position.

'That looks fine!' said Mac. 'Now I guess you'll be getting a bit tired, so you can take your leg home to get used to it. I want you to practise donning it, wearing it for a short time, and then doffing it again. Do that two or three times a day, and when you come back we can move on to the next stage.'

'Fine,' said Hannah, hiding her frustration behind defiance, and suppressing her need to burst into tears as her expectations of the leg crumbled. 'I think I'll take it off to go home,' she said.

Mac produced a bag in which the prosthesis could travel incognito, and Frankie took charge of it.

Hannah checked herself over and stood on her crutches ready to leave. 'Thank you so much for all your trouble!' she said to Mac, feeling consciously polite in the face of her disappointment.

'Don't mention it,' he said. 'Now, I'd like you to come in next week ...'

'Would Wednesday afternoon be OK? I'll have to see how it goes – I should be able to get in about half four.'

'Fine. I just need to see how you're getting on ... [he gave her yet another supposedly helpful prosthesis booklet, which Frankie took charge of] ... how you're going. I know I can trust you ...'

'Thanks.'

'Don't hesitate to give us a call if you have any problems – any problems at all. We're here to help ... not exactly 24/7, but you can always leave a message on the machine and we'll get back to you ... OK?'

'OK ... Right, we're off. Thanks again ...'

Hannah crutched out to freedom, enjoying the sunshine and fresh air in contrast to the atmosphere in the limb-fitting centre.

When she got home, Hannah made her way to the kitchen to be met by her mum: 'Where's the leg?' she asked.

Hannah slumped at the table, put her head in her hands and burst into tears of anger and frustration: 'Frank's got it,' she wept, 'You've no idea how terrible that session was,' she wept to her mum.

'Absolutely excruciating,' said Frankie, speaking for Hannah. 'I just don't know ...'

'I don't think I'm ever going to go back there,' said Hannah. 'I can't imagine how anyone can get a leg that fits perfectly, without any aches and pains, and then learn to walk on it as though it were her own.'

'It takes for ever to don the leg, and then you don't know whether it's right or not,' said Frankie, continuing the tale. 'And then it isn't right in one way or another and Mac takes it away for an hour to adjust it, and brings it back, and then it's wrong in a different way, and he's off again ...'

'Sounds like a nightmare,' said Jill sympathetically. 'But I suppose it's early days. Did you say you've got the leg Frankie? May I have a look?'

They went through to the sitting room and Frankie produced the leg: 'It weighs a ton, and looks like ... nothing on earth,' she said.

'And I've got to practise donning it, wearing it a bit, and then doffing it, before my next visit,' sniffed Hannah. 'I just don't know ...'

Jill took the leg, amazed at its weight, and examined it: 'So how do you put it on?' she asked.

'Aha! Is that a trick question?' asked Hannah. Even so, she took the leg and made to put it on. 'I push my stump into the socket here,' she demonstrated. 'You see? Then they ask how it feels, and I have no idea how it *ought* to feel.' She sat with the leg in position for a bit, and then removed it with an 'Ouch!'

'Nice when you stop,' she said. 'Like hitting yourself on the head with a brick.'

# 15
## Tom Curtis

om had just finished a swimming session at the Golden Splash. The bright sunshine warmed his toned skin and, on an impulse, he decided to change his route home to the one he had avoided since Hannah's accident – he'd cycle along the Tamthorpe Road.

Reaching the crucial spot, he propped his bike against the wall near where he'd left it on that dreadful day; he closed his eyes and stood and relived the moment when he had seen the E-butterfly lorry receding. Once again, he saw Hannah lying in the road, and was overcome with feelings of giddiness, nausea, and shame.

He felt ashamed that, having accompanied Hannah to the hospital after the accident, he had then deserted her, and hadn't contacted her since. He suddenly had a burning desire to see her again, apologise for his churlish behaviour, and hope that he might be forgiven, one way or another. Further, he hoped that they might again become as close as they had been before.

He reached the little area of grass at the end of Hannah's close, stood his bike against the rather worn bench seat with its strange nameplate – *Erected In Memory of Matthew Armitage (1912–1986) Benefactor, who loved to sit here* – and as ever wondered: what did Mr Armitage sit on before the bench was Erected in his Memory? Tom wiped the leaves off the seat before sitting down to consider what he might say to Hannah should he see her.

He suddenly realised that in reality he knew nothing of her new life. He had never seen her up and about with only one leg. How did she get about? Wheelchair? Crutches? Had she been fitted with a fake leg yet? What did that look like?

Then he relived so much of what they'd done together,

convinced that he could now accept Hannah in her present form – whatever it might be – and turn back the clock to their happy life before the accident. He was sure they could return to it – with some adjustments, of course.

Hesitantly, he wondered if – hoped that – Hannah might be ready to take up again from where they had so suddenly left off. Could she have moved on irrevocably, finding another soulmate, striking Tom out of her mind, never to consider all that they had shared in the fourteen or so years that they had lived alongside one another? How much had he lost touch with her everyday life? What had he actually missed?

Even as he pondered, Hannah's mum Jill appeared on her venerable old bicycle with its capacious basket, just as he remembered it. She saw Tom sitting on the bench, waved, and made her way over to see him; she seemed to be no different from before. Had Hannah changed? He had no way of knowing.

'Tom, dearest! Haven't seen you for such a long time … We've missed you so much … May I join you?'

She came and sat down on the bench, waiting for Tom to speak. There was a long silence while Tom wondered what to say, a jumble of thoughts racing through his mind.

At last: 'Oh Mrs Brooks – Jill – I've been such a fool … [Jill waited while Tom thought what to say] … Do you think Hannah might ever forgive me for deserting her? Has she … moved on? Found another … ? How is she anyway?' Screwing up his courage further, he asked: 'How's she getting on with only one leg?' He seemed to fight back tears as Jill made to give him a hug. He stiffened, wondering what Jill thought of him.

Jill continued to wait; she had some idea that Hannah was very taken with Ben, the boy she'd met in hospital; he'd brought her home on his motorbike once, but she had little idea of how her daughter currently viewed him – or how she viewed her erstwhile boyfriend Tom, for that matter.

Wondering what she should say – if she should say anything – she ventured: 'I know that Hannah has made some new friends … As for her leg … it's healing very well, and she's started on the road to a prosthesis, but she's still using her crutches rather than any other method to get about.

As she spoke, Jill heard a familiar muted sound of Hannah's crutches on the grass approaching.

Hannah had no sooner started out to the shops than she saw her mum sitting on the bench comforting someone who could only be Tom. She changed direction and quickened her step towards them, eager to find out what – or whom – they were talking about.

Tom emerged from Jill's arms to find Hannah sitting next to him, wearing the same thick green jumper and blue denim trousers that he remembered so well: 'Hannah Caramba!' he exploded, happiness seeping through his veins at the sight of her.

Hannah decided to play it cool: 'Hi, Tom,' she said, 'long time no see. How ya doin'?'

Jill released the boy and stood up diplomatically: 'Must get on with my shopping now, if you don't mind,' she said, extricating her bicycle and waving goodbye: 'Lovely to see you Tom. See you when I get back – I hope.'

' 'Byeee,' ' they responded in unison.

'Nice day for hanging out,' ventured Tom. 'What shall we do?'

'Hang out,' suggested Hannah. 'Have a catchup? Massive catchup?'

'OK,' smiled Tom. He sensed that something big could be about to happen to both of them.

'Come here,' laughed Hannah, leaning over and reaching out for him.

Tom laughed too; as they hugged each other, they appreciated what they had so missed over the past weeks.

Now that they were together, Hannah wanted to find out how much Tom might wish to link up with her again – or was he just being polite? And how did she herself really feel about the relationship?

Choosing her words carefully, Hannah said: 'Guess we might think about taking up swimming together again.' Tom's heart leapt. She continued: 'I've been thinking I ought to, but I've rather let it slide. Have you been keeping up with it?'

'Oh yeah! I certainly have, and what's more, I've got a marvellous new coach called Will Meredith. You should see him in the pool. Great movement.'

'I must say I haven't been swimming much recently, but I have been in the water at the ozzy therapy pool once or twice, just to make sure that I don't go round and round in circles, as some people suggested. And I'd certainly like to meet your Will Meredith. Do you think he could help me?'

'Sure he could – if he decides you've got what it takes, and he agrees to take you on. You could come to the pool with me tomorrow – 10 o'clock-ish – if that's OK.'

'Oh, that's great. Unfortunately, they don't have Paralympic diving – yet. I don't know what the prob might be. Getting up to the board, maybe. Perhaps Will could help. Now ... [no use beating about the bush] ... have you managed to accept the fact that I'm an O-L-er?'

'What's that? Oh, a one-legger? I think what I was afraid of was that ... Oh, I don't know what it was ... I just couldn't get my head round it ... such a change ... I'm really sorry. I don't know what I could – or couldn't – have been thinking of. It's so good just to be with you again. Can we put my ... lapse behind us? How've you been? You don't seem to have got yourself a fake leg yet. Are you going to?'

'I've recently started visiting the prosthetic clinic, and I've been measured and copied ...'

'Copied?'

Hannah laughed at the evident confusion on Tom's face.

'Yes. They make a plaster replica of your stump, so they can fit the socket of the prosthesis to it when you're not there. By the way, I hope you're cool with the word "stump". Some people go all squeamish about it ... we could always say "residual limb".'

Tom nodded hesitantly '... I think I can manage ...'

'So they've made me my first prosthetic leg, but I don't like it very much – in fact I don't like it at all – and I still prefer to use my crutches to get about. But of course I have to use the fake leg when I go to the clinic, or there'd be no point in going. But what I really want to do of course is to get the leg working comfortably – end of.'

Hannah stooped, retrieved her crutches, and stood up straight in front of Tom looking at him intently. For the very first time, he saw her properly standing on her one leg supported on her crutches and appreciated how her short stump enabled her left trouser-leg to be folded up sharply and secured behind her.

'Wow!' said Tom appreciatively, 'That looks so neat.'

'I've got Frankie to thank for that,' said Hannah. 'I decided what I wanted, and she's worked hard on getting it exactly right for me. Really square crease.'

Tom thought with a pang that he hadn't been any help to Hannah at all. 'Do you have a wheelchair?' he asked. 'I could always push you places to be friendly.' He thought he'd better not go too far at this early stage.

'I do have a wheelchair,' said Hannah, 'but I avoid it if I can. It does seem so huge. And then you'd be leaning over me to make sure that I could hear what you were saying.'

'Umm ... Well, what shall we do now, then?'

'Why not come round mine, now you're here?' suggested Hannah.

Tom caught his breath as the possibility of making amends for what he now saw as his lapse loomed larger. He retrieved his bicycle and wheeled it slowly beside Hannah as she crutched along. Tom realised that this was the first time he had actually seen her progressing in this way, and though he was devastated by her loss, he couldn't help admiring her crutching skill.

Hannah led him up her drive and through to the garden, where they settled in a sunny spot as in days of old. Tom was excited at returning to once-familiar territory, but fearful of doing or saying something that would break the spell, and ruin what they had just started re-establishing.

He sat back and looked at Hannah carefully, continuing to get used to her new appearance. As far as he could see, the only difference between the Hannah of old and the Hannah of today (apart from the tell-tale crutches) was the altered leg of her jeans. He couldn't imagine why he had been so repelled by the idea of seeing her.

'How long did it take you to get used to having one leg?' he asked.

'I'm not sure that you ever get used to it,' said Hannah. 'But, yes, I feel more and more used to it as I get to do everyday things without having to think about them in great detail beforehand. You'd be amazed how tasks such as washing your face, or making toast, break down into so many little steps.'

Tom thought about that. 'So, what else has been happening?' he asked.

'Oh Tom ...' Hannah began, pouring out accounts of what she had been doing and who she had met, as in the old days. Tom absorbed everything as he used to, when Hannah would chatter on with little pause. It dawned on him that since her accident Hannah had met a completely new raft of people and had had a far more exciting time than he had. Now she was talking about Lorna Macey and her grandmother Delia Winchester.

'... In later years, she'd lived in this big house with her granny who'd become an O-L-er at the start of the Second World War. And when her granny died, Lorna inherited the house and her granny's formidable collection of O-L things – crutches, legs, books and so on – and she's been having a clear-out and downsizing, which is why she recently passed on her whole collection to me and I've now got it all up in my room. She wanted to find an interested person who would keep the whole collection together. And I must say I've found a real interest in all this historical O-L stuff. Would you like to see it?'

'Yes *please*,' said Tom enthusiastically, though it did sound a bit bizarre and out-of-the-blue.

They went up to Hannah's room, just as in the old days, although now Tom watched carefully how Hannah negotiated the stairs with both ocelots in her left hand and her right hand on the rail.

Tom admired Hannah's new cupboards with framed photographs neatly fastened to the doors – Delia on the Lady Ms, and Lady M herself on her ride-on lawnmower.

Hannah stood her ocelots aside, got out the Lady Ms and slipped them under her arms to show Tom how special they were.

'They're very beautiful,' he admired, 'but they do look rather … old-fashioned.'

'That's the very point,' said Hannah. 'My usual ozzy issue crutches are modern elbow, or forearm, crutches – in fact I hardly knew about this sort at all – these are axilla crutches – axilla's the armpit – and I've been finding out all about them – they've long gone out of fashion – in this country, certainly – mainly, I think, because they're too inflexible – particularly on stairs. Would you like to try what they feel like?'

Tom took the Lady Ms and placed them under his arms. It was a first for him and it opened his eyes to some of what crutch-users of old had had to contend with. He took a few steps; it felt very strange, copying Hannah, but made him feel much closer to her, and what she had to go through.

Then Hannah passed Tom a pair of elbow crutches and took the Lady Ms herself.

Tom tried the elbow crutches and tuned back into Hannah's comments: 'I see what you mean about flexible and inflexible. These feel far more … safe …'

'Yes. On the other hand,' continued Hannah, 'axillary crutches make it possible for you to walk on a single crutch and, if you're lucky, you can use your stump to help the crutch move so that you're hands free. In fact, I'm thinking about writing an article about walking on crutches because there's so much to say – but I don't know who might be interested when I've said it.'

Tom realised that he was on the brink of becoming privy to intimate details of Hannah's new life, the like of which he could never have imagined: 'So what about *those* crutches, then?'

He drew Hannah's attention to the pictures on the door.

'This picture is Lorna's granny Delia supported on this very pair of Lady Ms I have here, and this picture is Lady Morris – or Lady M – on her lawnmower. It was she who gave the Lady Ms to Delia. And that's why they're called "Lady Ms". Even the Queen saw her on them.'

'Wow! So what other interesting things have you acquired?'

Hannah pulled out Delia's original battered old pair of crutches, handling them fondly and carefully: 'Delia lost her leg in the Coventry air raid when the City and its Cathedral were destroyed – 1940 – and it was her thirteenth birthday, so she became an amputee on the same day on which she became a teenager. And here are the crutches she was first given in hospital, with no instruction or explanation of how to use them. They were so important to Delia.'

Next, Hannah went to a different part of the cupboard and pulled out the original pegleg that the village basketmaker had made for Delia. As always when she held the Fisher pegleg she was acutely aware of handling a unique piece of folk art that had meant everything to a young girl injured during the War. She handed it to Tom: 'This must be one of the most interesting pieces in the collection,' she said.

Tom took it and held it and turned it over and over as he studied it. 'Wow!' he said. 'If I'm not mistaken, it's an artificial leg – a wooden leg – that presumably belonged to Delia. And it's made of woven canes sprouting out of a bamboo.'

'Got it in one,' laughed Hannah. 'Made for the young Delia by the village basketmaker way back in 1940. Making use of the material and techniques he knew best. You push your stump in here.' She decided to say nothing about her trying the leg on. She felt that that should stay private – at least for the time being. She hadn't even mentioned it to her family yet.

⁂

As time passed, it struck Tom that for Hannah to be so openly comfortable with him was both an invitation for him to return to their previous intimacy and an acknowledgement that such a thing was possible.

Hannah herself was convinced that Tom would have to have an opportunity of meeting her stump before he and she could be fully reunited, but she didn't want to make too a big thing of it.

When Tom excused himself from the room for a moment, she swiftly changed into her frilly denim skirt, and when he returned, she was sitting on the edge of her bed – cool, calm and collected – ready to show him.

'Now ... perhaps you'd care to look at me ... to find out what I look like now?' challenged Hannah, a glint in her eye.

'I guess I can be that brave,' said Tom, somewhat surprised but truly pleased at Hannah's invitation. 'It'll never be any worse than now, will it?'

He sat on her left and summoned up the courage to explore her stump: 'Crinkly,' he said with surprise. 'Does it … hurt?'

'I get phantom feelings sometimes,' said Hannah. 'That's when you think you have feelings in a bit of you that isn't actually there any more. And there are shooting pains in the stump from time to time. But now it's generally a lot better than it has been. And surely better than you might think, judging from its … crinkliness.'

'I'm pleased to hear that,' Tom said. 'Do you think it'll ever …?' But then they were interrupted by Jill calling them down for lunch.

Hannah and her sisters were really glad to see Tom at the table again. His presence somehow restored an easiness that seemed to have been missing from the Brooks household since the day of the accident. They had so much to talk about – but there was scarcely any mention of Tom's having being absent, and no one made a great thing of Hannah's accident.

Before he left, Olivia invited Tom to a concert she was singing in … just like old times.

'So … do you think Tom's going to come back into your life?' probed Frankie tentatively.

Hannah laughed: 'I think he already has,' she said. 'There seems to be no good reason that kept him away, and he's supercool with O-L me, and he's met my stump without freaking out, so that's about it.'

'I've been thinking,' said Frankie.

'Careful,' said Hannah, 'what?'

'It's Tom's birthday the Tuesday after next. 'Spose you take him to the movies and then we all meet at The Khyber for a secret curry?'

'OK … and invite the gang, eh?'

'Sounds perfect. Something to look forward to.'

The following morning, Tom came over to Hannah again to continue their catch-up, drawn to her as if by magnetic force. He'd seen her collection of O-L things, and he'd met her crinkly stump, but they hadn't yet talked about her artificial leg.

More confident than the previous day, he broached the burning subject again: 'So, what exactly are you doing about getting a fake leg?' he asked.

Unfazed, Hannah went to her cupboard and produced the leg that Mac had made: 'This is it,' she said, slightly awkwardly. 'Umm … feel it.'

'That's … *huge*,' said Tom.

'Quite a surprise?' laughed Hannah.

Somewhat gingerly, Tom took hold of the leg around the knee joint beneath the socket and tried its weight: 'Wow!' he said, 'that's pretty heavy.'

'That's what everyone says,' said Hannah, 'it's huge, it's heavy, and what do you do with a thing like that?'

Tom couldn't think of a sensitive answer, so matter-of-factly he looked at the foot: 'Well, judging by the foot, the leg seems to go this way round, so I suppose your stump goes into the socket – here – is that it?'

'Yes, technically, that's right. In effect, I sit on here … [Hannah demonstrated how the socket fitted on to her stump and she sat on the edge] … so I don't put any pressure on the end of the stump itself. First I put the leg on – that's donning it; then I'm supposed to wear it for a bit, and then I can take it off again – that's doffing it.

That's my homework until the next session at Jimmy's. Mr Peters the consultant said I had to keep donning it, and then wearing it for a bit, before doffing it. You might think I couldn't wait to get a prosthesis, but now we've got to the point where I've found what it's like, I'm a bit less than keen.'

'Some sort of prob?'

'Huge … the prosthesis never seems to fit as well as I'm sure it ought to, and so I try it on, and it feels wrong somewhere, so then they spend ages adjusting it, and I try it on again and it hurts in different places, and even worse when I get it home. So I much prefer to use my crutches for the time being. They're not as awkward as you might think. But I'm sure we'll get the leg right in the end, even if they have to make me another socket.'

'Sounds awful …'

'Yes, and there are rumblings about what's possible as opposed to what's available. I've met several other amputees at physio, and there's a general feeling that the best prosses ought to be available on the NHS.'

'Are they not, then?'

'No. It seems that some military amputees have better replacement legs available, acknowledging their sacrifice for their country. But there's an ex-fireman called Stan who I've met at physio, and he gets quite hot under the collar because he can't see why the leg he sacrificed for his community isn't just as important as a soldier's sacrificial leg. And the military have recently been awarded another few million quid specially to buy the very latest prosses. And legs are getting better and better. The latest thing is what's called the Genium leg. By monitoring the movements of parts of the leg, there's a microprocessor that can understand what you want to do much quicker than you can. The blurb says the Genium leg contains an accelerometer and a gyroscope and makes it easier to walk over uneven ground, or to walk backwards, or up and down stairs, leg over leg …'

'So these wonderful legs exist, but aren't available on the NHS?' said Tom. 'Doesn't seem fair to me, especially when what is available is so pants – as your experience shows.'

'Doesn't seem fair to lots of other people either, especially amputees who are having experiences similar to mine. And another thing: the military have their wonderful residential rehab facility at Headley Court with a full structured rehab programme, whereas plebs like me get one physio session a week if we're lucky. But don't let me get carried away …'

'Haven't I seen amputees appealing to raise funds to buy an upmarket pros?' asked Tom. 'Perhaps we could set out on that path.'

'We could, but we'd need lots more funds beyond the cost of one pros – to keep it in good repair and supply renewals for life. Mum knows Vanessa Telford of the *Chronicle*, who has offered to get something going when I feel ready. But as things are, everything points to me staying on crutches – for the time being at any rate. We'll see …'

ℬↄ

'So what am I going to wear for this birthday trip to CineWorld?' asked Hannah, looking into her wardrobe. 'Trousers or skirt?'

Frankie thought deeply. 'Well, I know you love your green trousers and spangly top? – I'll help you with the trouser-leg.'

'OK. And my strappy green shoe. That should strike the right note. And if I wear it, would you like to paint my toe-nails green for me please?'

To complete the look, Hannah extracted a pair of sparkly green elbow crutches from Delia's hoard. Excited by her new ensemble, she went to show her mum. 'Wait there,' said Jill.

Feeling like a fashion model being prepared for a show, Hannah waited while Jill promptly fetched a couple of loose, filmy scarves in shades of green shot with silver, which she draped round her daughter to set off the rest of the outfit perfectly.

'How about that?' asked Jill.

Hannah looked at herself in the long hall mirror, and for once her mum's suggestion was just right. Now, she felt ready for Tom and the cinema – and whatever might come after it.

There was a scrunching of gravel as Tom arrived and jumped out of the car looking as immaculately casual as did Hannah.

'Stunning,' said Tom enthusiastically.

'Not bad yourself,' said Hannah.

Arriving at the cinema car park, Tom made for the disabled spaces near to the entrance, thinking that this would soon become second nature. Almost immediately, a jobsworth appeared from nowhere: ''Ere, you can't park there without a permit.'

'I'm afraid I don't have a permit,' apologised Tom, 'but I do have a disabled passenger. Surely that's OK? After all, it's not exactly full …'

By this time, Hannah had emerged from the car and, rather than retrieving her ocelots, hopped round to face the jobsworth with an enchanting smile on her face: 'You wouldn't want me to have to hop further than I need to?' she asked him meltingly.

Taken aback by this sudden confrontation with a one-legged girl: 'J-j-just this once – without a p-p-permit,' he stuttered, and disappeared into the shadows. Grinning to herself, Hannah retrieved her ocelots from the back seat.

Tom noticed that Hannah turned a few heads as she swung along and, not for the first time, he reflected how physically – and mentally – tiring walking on crutches must be.

Some people openly stared, making him feel more protective towards Hannah. He broached the subject.

'Well, first of all, I'm used to it,' said Hannah, brushing off Tom's concern. 'And of course I've got to get on with it anyway – otherwise, how do I get along? It's OK because I'm quite slim, and the leg that's gone weighed a few pounds, so I'm lighter than you might think, and my arms are getting stronger by the day. So *pleeease* don't worry; it's how I am.'

Tom pressed on: 'If you deigned to use a wheelchair,' he said, 'I could push you ... and it would be interesting to see if people would stare more or less,'

Hannah shuddered. 'Some people love a wheelchair, and use it as if it were a pros. But ... I don't know ... I'm a crutch person. Independent. I'd only use a wheelchair if I absolutely had to. It feels like such a huge structure compared with a couple of sticks'

'I see what you mean,' said Tom, pleased to find himself moving into Hannah's world. 'On crutches, you can talk to people at their own level, and look less ... different than if you were sitting in a wheelchair.'

As they made their way to the ticket desk, a small neat girl in an usherette's tabard appeared: 'Excuse me ...'

'Yes?' said Hannah warily, wondering if there were some health and safety bar to people on crutches entering the auditorium, but the girl addressed Tom: 'Hi, I'm Dawn. Are you this lady's carer?'

Surprised, Tom thought quickly: 'Yes,' he said.

'Come with me, then,' said Dawn, 'it's two for the price of one – disabled person and carer. Half price each. Which film would you like to see?'

' '*Green Awakening*,' ' they said together.

'Good,' said Dawn. 'You'll be able to see the movie in the de luxe auditorium with complimentary drinks and popcorn.' She led the way and ushered them in: 'I'll look after everything for you,' she said. 'Where would you like to sit?'

Hannah pointed to where they always used to like sitting – the middle of the back section.

'Now,' said Dawn, 'if you'd come in a wheelchair you could've sat down there.' She indicated a space right at the front of the auditorium.

'Thanks,' said Hannah 'I'll remember that ...' adding under her breath '... if ever I want to get a crick in the neck.'

Tom made his way up the stairs grinning, proud that Hannah – his Hannah – was so independent. He marvelled at her confident agility as she made for her chosen seat and stowed her crutches. Dawn brought the refreshments, and they settled down to enjoy the film.

✍

The closing titles rolled to swelling music and the audience stood, ready for the rush to the exit.

Hannah leant towards Tom: 'Let them go,' she said. 'It'll make it easier for me.'

So they sat, hands touching, chatting about the film until the crowd had dispersed; then Hannah retrieved her crutches and started to swing her way down the stairs. Tom was once again amazed by her sure-footedness.

✍

In the foyer, Hannah suggested they go to eat at the Khyber, to celebrate both Tom's birthday, and their renewed relationship. Tom had no idea that the old gang would be there too. Like Hannah, he felt deliriously happy.

## Publishers' note

Rather than leave Hannah with an unsatisfactory leg, we intend to visit her again to continue our report on her life and progress.

If you have any points you would like the new narrative to consider addressing, please send them to us by e-mail at hannah.brooks@fernhouse.com, or by post to
Fern House
19 High Street
Haddenham
ELY
Cambs CB6 3XA.

We will be very pleased to hear from you.